Stealing Andrew Jackson's Head

A Novel Based on the Life of Captain S.W. Dewey

Charles D. Rodenbough

Technical Consultant: Ryan Ray Rodenbough

For Dr. John Ryan Rodenbough

and Dr. Danielle Ray –

the middle generation.

The author is seventy-eight.
The consultant is his grandson, age twelve.
If you are old, think of the reflective face of a twelve-year-old.
If you are young, think what memories you will someday have.
Value them both respectfully.
The green leaf will surely turn to the yellow of autumn,
And in the spring will come again.

Chapter One

My Father was a Sea Captain

The leaves blowing in a funnel in front of his small transom window caused Samuel to look up. He saw Mrs. Albright before she pulled open his heavy door and began descending the steps into his small room. He had a moment to prepare before, like the blustering wind which accompanied her arrival, she swirled into his presence with purpose.

"Good morning, dear lady," he got off quickly to cushion her determination. He was also trying to recall her first name.

"Samuel, it is not enough to greet me with such casual good humor," she began. "You left the house again without your breakfast, and I cannot continue to take up my day bringing your meals over here when your place is regularly set with the other tenants."

He stared at her—confused. "My breakfast? I had my breakfast—as usual."

"You forgot your breakfast—as usual."

"My dear Lydia." He was relieved to recall her name. "If again I neglected to take my place at your most robust table, I humbly apologize. I find myself forgetting the date and having to look at the masthead of the *Enquirer* each morning to start my day," he said with a submissive tilt of his head that masked his true concern about his failing memory.

"It is Thursday, February fourth, eighteen ninety-six, and don't tell me you do not remember your own birthday." She was scolding but she too was masking concerns.

She pushed aside some of his books and papers scattered upon the table he used for a desk and set the covered tray she had been carrying on it. He caught himself in a reactive move to protest her rearrangement of his papers and dropped his shoulders in a subjective act of surrender.

"Now here, sit before it chills further. I am sure that your eggs will have cooled but your scrapple will still be warm." She stepped away from the desk signaling for him to sit.

As Mrs. Albright hovered, he ate his breakfast obediently and vaguely recalled as he did that he had come straight over to his office after he had dressed. Breakfast had not even occurred to him. Had he avoided the meal, or the conversation with that odd collection of dim personalities who shared rooms at 23 Fifth Street—*Fiddler's Rest*?

"I do appreciate your kindness, Lydia. I must disrupt your day. It seems that I am caught up in so many projects that I must surely press forward or leave them unfinished in the end."

"Today you have attained your ninth decade, Samuel. We all admire you for it and I dare say we are all a little jealous. Is it too much to expect a little wandering of the mind at such an age? Small price, I'd say."

Samuel wondered, why did people discount his frustration? He could sense their unease—their clear recognition that his attention wandered as he talked. He admitted that he would find himself standing in a place without knowing why he was there. He told others things, and they would say that he never had. He kept a dictionary at hand in his office, and a Thesaurus, because he forgot the spelling of some words and, when he tried to pull out a particular word, he had to start with synonyms and agitate his brain to search for the word he needed. It seemed always to take longer and when he was speaking, he found himself hung on the search for a word, his mind whirling, struggling for context. His listener perceived he was in some kind of reverie but his mind was contesting for an index. Small wonder that he was more at ease when he was alone? When it was his own thoughts that stimulated his mind, he still found himself stuck on a word but his mind was struggling with itself. Another thought might carry him away in another direction but it was his direction and he did not have to apologize or feel embarrassment.

"By the way," he said with a confident countenance looking up at her. "I am entering my tenth decade with my ninetieth year."

"You are indeed," Lydia broke in, "and you don't seem to have lost your appetite with age."

He realized she was taking up the tray. "Oh, yes I still like to eat—when I remember to do so." He managed a weak smile. "Thank you so much. Could I survive without you?"

"I have answered that question more than once in my life," she said with an equally wan smile. "My second husband claimed I was indispensable to him until he left with Mistress Sally Fern. A woman's life is filled with dependent men and when she dies, they survive."

He feared she would settle to engage him in another recitation of her "three worthless husbands," but not this day. As she turned to climb the stairs, the heavy door, buffeted by the blustering wind struggling with young Jake Cooper's efforts to pry it open, sucked in a spray of debris. Mrs. Albright's face screwed into a contortion and her left elbow flew up to block the gust. "Jake, you are bringing in half the trash of Philadelphia. Here, hold the door and let me out." She pushed up the stairs and through the door with a protest, "Oh my!"

"Come in, Jake. I have something more for you to take to the printer."

Jake Cooper was more than just an errand-boy for Samuel. They were attached to each other "with hoops of steel." The boy was eleven. His father had died in a tavern brawl and left Jake, his mother and little sister on their own. They had taken two rooms at the *Fiddler's Rest* a few years earlier. Jake had been especially lonely, until that day when he had followed Samuel the two blocks to his basement hide-a-way under the "Shipman's Guild." The first time he had only watched from across the street. When he followed Samuel a second day, he peered in the corner of the small window, but the old man had observed his presence. That night at the table, Samuel had made a point of seating himself by the boy and, without calling attention, asked if Jake would like to accompany him the next day. Jake had said he would, but secretly the boy had some fear about this place where Samuel went each morning. He was even a little uneasy about the old man himself. Samuel did not know why he had suggested that the boy join him—an impulse but from some feeling that it might be rewarding.

After breakfast the next day Samuel and Jake had walked together neither saying anything, only fulfilling an arrangement. The street outside the entrance to the basement stairs led down to the Delaware River where a collection of masts bobbed and rolled. The wind was usually gusty off the water. Many of the shops along this street, and all the warehouses, had some connection with commerce or the shipping fleet. Upper floors above stores were often rented for the accommodation or satisfaction of seamen. That made the street boisterous after dark but very pleasant during the day. Quartered under the "Shipman's Guild,"

Samuel had little worry that his basement room, filled with the treasures of his life, would be violated.

The entrance jutted out from the brick building. Samuel had a very large key that he had struggled to work into the lock when Jake followed him next morning to the room. Jake had waited, idly studying the entrance as Samuel fumbled. The door had opened onto the descending stairs which were covered by a rounded roof, tied back into the face of the guild building and walled with the same brick. It was dingy-dark, the only light at first coming from the four panes of the window. At the bottom of the stairs, Samuel had turned on the two ceiling bulbs, adding considerable brightness to the room.

"Welcome, Jake," the old man had said, his voice softened by exertion. "This is where I come every day. I call it my office, but just between us, it is my treasure house." His manner was slyly conspiratorial. The boy had scanned the room as Samuel continued. "Not many have been down here, boy, and I want to keep it that way. You must promise me right now, that you will not tell your friends about anything you see here. Don't brag about what you know and certainly don't speak to any strangers that might have unworthy interests in my collection. Do you understand?"

Jake's nod had reflected his divided attention as he noticed objects of interest. His young mind struggled to take seriously the obligation Samuel had placed before him. His first reaction indeed had been to think who he might tell. Samuel, however, had turned Jake's emerging knowledge into a trust. He had never been party to a real trust—with consequences. "Yes, sir," he'd replied. "I understand. I can keep a secret. I won't tell no one."

Samuel had not meant to bind him to such an ironclad understanding but had figured it wouldn't hurt for the time being if that was how Jake had interpreted the arrangement. It would ease Samuel's concerns. The old man had puttered about a bit, lit two candles on a table. Jake had thought that strange when he had two good electric lights. Samuel had explained that for most of his years he had written by candle-light and he felt "bulb-light" alone cast a kind of glare that was irritating. "Newfangled," he'd said for the first of many times that Jake would hear that term of judgment.

Jake's young brown eyes had continued to sweep the room like search-lights. Except under the window, the room was walled with shelves which in turn were cluttered in random rows of books, stacks of writing papers, and rolls of larger sheets of papers the boy thought were maps. On one wall there was a strange fireplace—a semi-circle of brick, an opening filled with burned coal, and a metal hood above. "I only use that in this time of year to take the chill off the room. In the winter, I keep a fire in it all the time."

There was a door opening on the back wall and a cord swung between two nails held up a tartan blanket that concealed the contents behind it. "This is my desk, Jake." It was a table, Jake could see, but he'd accept it as a desk. "I have been many places in my life and I have done many things. Some I am proud of and some, not so." The casual confession was lost on Jake.

That is how their companionship had begun, with Samuel encouraging some rules and Jake's timid acknowledgment that he was hooked. A bridge had appeared, not yet stout, between a boy and an old man, connecting a yearning need each sheltered in his own heart.

The first day the two just talked about things—mostly themselves. Samuel had much more to tell and Jake was an earnest listener. They discovered almost immediately that they shared enquiring minds—even though they came to that understanding of their relationship from a wide difference in perspectives. It took a few days for Jake to overcome his awe of Samuel and his "treasures". He had never *known* an old man. All adults he thought of as old. Old meant removed from what Jake knew, living, but somewhere else—not now. As if by measure, Jake became conscious that Samuel was emerging as a category of person who gave significance to "old." He had to observe, then overcome, Samuel's slower movements—his sometimes halting speech, the words he used that Jake had never heard used before, even simple words. He sometimes caught himself studying Samuel's skin, his milky eyes, his yellow teeth. He had a different smell, not unpleasant, but like . . . with the room. At first he seemed to have to go through each fresh observation in its newness, examining it, trying to place it with something he already knew. After a week, he had pushed that aside. He still processed the new things he observed about Samuel and his treasures but back somewhere, behind the next thing or beyond the words Samuel was speaking. He liked to hear Samuel speak. The old man's voice put Jake at ease. Somehow he soon knew Samuel's words were important and what he was being told was very special. One day he thought, He speaks to me, not like I am a boy, but as someone with whom he wants to share his special things. Jake was puzzled. He was also pleased. Why has he chosen me? Should I know such things? If they are special, and I am a boy, is it right that I should understand?

In the first weeks Samuel also had strange and sometimes obtuse thoughts. Am I so shallow that I am reduced to confiding myself, my things, to this boy? Have I become so simple, so needy? I should be committing these things to paper. They are important. I should be important. Instead, I am so reduced that at the end I must entrust my discoveries, my treasures, my life, to a boy. I should get a dog.

Such early struggles soon faded. He lost the need to justify or find explanations. He was overcome with the natural comfort with which this relationship seemed to take possession of his spirit. This bond simply was, and he needed nothing more to explain it.

Now, like most boys of his age, Jake was prone to use the one word question, *why?* When he was confused or when he suspected more than he understood, *why* was a protective challenge that he could project. It was his idiomatic context for an inquiring mind. *Why?* Right away, he recognized that it was not an expression he could use with an old man. When he or his friends used it with each other, it was a way of saying -- *explain yourself or I won't believe it*. When he said *why* to his mother, he meant he needed to know more. When he said *why* to Samuel, it was like a betrayal of a confidence, or a sharp reminder that the confidence might have been wasted on a boy. He had observed how Samuel had slightly winced, sometimes startled to a stop like a horse responding to the sudden pull of reins. He promised himself to stop using *why*. It took him a while to find the right substitute.

Samuel also knew this relationship needed a little grooming, a little cultivation. All his life he had been attracted to people who had those inquiring minds. For him it had become the context of two people, before he had always meant adults, who listened in proportion to speaking and who had knowledge sufficient to the conversation. He put no conditions on the acquisition of knowledge. An academic could be as wise or as foolish as a subsistence farmer. At some point in the first week he applied that definition to Jake and ever afterwards the boy satisfied the measure.

In fits and starts Samuel tested the role, as a teacher, parent, confidant, master. Some played better than others, but neither model seemed to have sustaining value. What indeed did he require in this relationship? If he could find that, perhaps that would also satisfy some of Jake's needs. After all, it was Jake's cup that was nearly empty and Samuel's that was full to overflowing.

That was it, Samuel thought. My problem is that my cup, my experience, my life, overflows and I have a need to share; but my friends are dead, my family is gone, and I no longer have any relevance. Once I was sought. I am wiser now than then. I have more treasures but no one is interested any more. I still have to pour out my cup but I have to find another that is nearly empty. And it can't be empty simply because it is not seeking. No, it has to be an eager receptacle, beginning to search, acceptable of someone else's contribution.

Jake could never have understood Samuel's musings. He might have understood the cup euphemism but what did it mean to be relevant? Jake's needs were more instinctive. His mind was searching. His appetite for knowledge was surging. Teachers measured out knowledge in equal spoonfuls. His mother provided knowledge for the role she expected him to assume. His friends shared ignorance more than knowledge and he had no like for adult knowledge that was always cautionary. But without being able to give it definition, it was his cup that needed to be filled.

And so it began. At first randomly—Samuel watching as Jake eased around the room, stopping with a questioning pause then moving on. Initially he would venture out with a finger and touch an object. Samuel never said, "Don't touch." Then he began to pick up objects and examine them in more detail. Samuel watched him without prompting. The first questions were not words but reflective touching or turning of something. Then Jake began to hold things up. He would cock his head to examine facets or to better see dimensions. After a few days, it was from Samuel that the first questions came.

"What does that feel like it might be, Jake?"

"It's a ball but it is the heaviest ball I ever picked up. A body couldn't play with it or it would bust something, that's for sure. Nearest thing I can say is it reminds me some of those things I saw hanging on each side of Missus Albright's windows that they called weights. I think they kept the window up when it was open in the summer. Could this be some kind of weight, Mister Dewey?"

"That's a good guess and a wise speculation. Can I tell you a story?"

"Yes sir."

"That is, I guess, one of the first things I collected in my life. You see, my father was a sea captain, and when I was born my family lived in the harbor town of Falmouth in Massachusetts. You know where Massachusetts is, don't you?"

"Yes sir, I do. We studied that in geography."

"Well, I know you know where Boston is, and when I was three my family moved there. Then when I was in my seventh year, the United States had its second war with England. I remember my father got very excited in those days every time an American sailing ship was boarded from a British ship and our sailors were impressed into the British navy. It was the tactic of a bully and it was against international laws on sailing rights. Of course Massachusetts, like Philadelphia, depended on the commerce of the sea so we were in direct competition with Britain for control of any part of the sea. Since my father was already a sea captain and he had his own ship, he and his ship were placed under command of the United States Navy. My father's name was Samuel, like mine, and he had a friend, another sea captain of the Navy from Rhode Island, named Christopher Raymond Perry. My father heard that Captain Perry's son, who was only about twenty-five, had himself become a Captain of the Navy. This young man had requested and received command of a small American fleet to guard Lake Erie. Young Perry had only a few ships and, in order to succeed in defending the lake, he built more ships at a place called Dobbin's Landing in Presque Isle Bay to match the British fleet on the lake. My father, although as I said he was a ship's captain, had been commissioned a Lieutenant in eighteen twelve, in the third regiment, U. S. Artillery, and then promoted to command at Fort Warren in Boston Harbor. I guess the Army thought a sailor would know all about artillery. When my father heard what young Oliver Hazzard Perry was doing at Lake Erie, he got permission to march his command there to help him build and arm his ships, since he was an older man and had much experience. He started overland but became very ill along the way and he died of dysentery at Sackett's Harbor in New York. I was my parent's oldest child and I had two sisters and a brother who was not even a year old. I know the most vivid memory of my childhood was that day when my grandpa came to our house to tell us that my daddy was dead. My mama cried so hard, it was like she would never be able to stop. And my sisters and my little brother cried because she was crying and I believed I couldn't cry because Grandpa was standing there so bewildered he didn't know what to do next. I told him it would be all right and I would hold my mother so she could stop crying and then he cried. I'm telling you this, Jake, because I know that your papa also died when you were not much older than I was when I lost my papa. We share a great sad experience in our lives. Perhaps we share a special sympathy that we don't have with everyone. We know what it is like to be without a father when a person is young. We know what the feeling of responsibility is like even before anybody ever told us about responsibility. A common event, at a similar age, forced us into an experience and duty before anyone else had prepared us. We had to find a way to do, before we could ask why."

Jake was looking at Samuel because he noticed there was something about the old man's words that shown through his face. He had never noticed that before in a person. He feared that if he spoke he might intrude some way but he felt it was important that he listen very hard. As the weeks went on, he often had this feeling deep down. What he was hearing was not just this old man talking like a lot of old men do. By the expression on his face and the gentleness with which Samuel seemed to be talking only to Jake, the boy experienced a sensitivity that he had not had before with anyone.

Samuel continued. "My grandfather was named Benoni. That is a very unusual name for a boy, don't you think?"

Jake nodded.

"It is from the Bible and it means 'son of my sorrow.' My grandpa was born eight days after his father had died so he was given that name by his grieving mother. So when my father died and I was still a young boy, Benoni could sympathize with me when I was sad. Grandpa was a blacksmith and he lived in Hanover in New Hampshire where there is the college named Dartmouth. Half a year after my father had died, Grandpa came to our house one day carrying that iron ball and he gave it to me. I thought he might have made it for me in his blacksmith's shop but he had not. You see, right after my father died, the fleet that young Captain Oliver Hazzard Perry had assembled on Lake Erie was attacked by a British fleet and the Americans won the Battle of Lake Erie. Perry became a national hero and a great hero in my life. I could imagine my father as the hero of that battle if only he had lived. I guess in my young mind that is how I made him by transfer even bigger in death than he had been in life. Can you understand? People do that some times. Captain Perry's flagship, the *USS Lawrence,* was destroyed and he had to transfer his command to the *USS Niagara.* His flag bore the words 'DON'T GIVE UP THE SHIP' and I could see my daddy carrying that flag in a small dingy from one ship to the other. When Captain Perry had won the battle he sent word to General William Henry Harrison, 'We have met the enemy and they are ours.'

Oliver Hazzard Perry at Battle of Lake Erie

"My friends and I used to play sailor by the hour and say over and over, 'Don't give up the ship' and 'We have met the enemy and they are ours.' My grandpa must have somehow known how I was mixing these events with the sorrow that I was feeling without a father, and he had contacted Captain Perry who had sent him a cannonball from the Battle of Lake Erie so he could give it to the son of another sea Captain who had died on his way to help him in battle."

Jake was looking down intently at the ball in his hands. "And this is it?" he said. "This is really the cannonball from the Battle of Lake Erie?"

"Yes it is, Jake, and when I die, if you like, that treasure will be yours. Now you better get on your way to the print shop with my article."

Chapter Two

Benoni Dewey

The boy did not come every day. Samuel did not want him to let the visits interfere with school or Jake's play with his friends. They had to be a natural part of the boy's activities or Samuel thought that he might tire and lose interest. The old man knew it would be up to him to sense how to balance their time together so that it did not become an obligation or, still worse, boring.

Samuel had seen that the time with Jake was more important to him than to the boy. He perceived that need and he was bothered. It had seemed demeaning at first, but then became disturbing. Was he trying to create something for himself in the boy? It wasn't an alter-ego. That was unnatural. That is when he envisioned the image of the two cups—one full and one yet empty. He would treat Jake more as an adult with a child's imagination. He wouldn't talk down to him as to a child, but on a more equal plane. He would let the objects in this place inspire the curiosity. Then Samuel would share the story, or a story from the circumstances that had originally inspired his own curiosity to percolate. If he had reckoned the boy correctly, their interests would mix, satisfying the want of each.

When Jake came down the stairs it was mid-afternoon. Samuel was working on his latest article for the *Philadelphia Inquirer*. He made a circular motion with his index finger, indicating to Jake that he should look around until he got to a stopping place. The boy never minded waiting because he believed he would never get through seeing everything Samuel had in this room.

Finally, Samuel put down his pen with a flourish as if he had just done something very important. "Well, my young friend, I see by the stain of grass on the back of your pants that you and your friends must have been playing war again or at least roughhousing. Am I right?"

"Yes, Mister Dewey. We did play pretty hard after lunch and a little just now, after school was out. I didn't know I had grass on my clothes. Should I go out and brush it off?"

"No! No!" "We'll count any grass that falls off as just another relic for the collection. Now tell me what has gone on in your life since last you were here. By the way, I wanted to explain that I try to not mention anything at the table at Missus Albright's about your coming here or what we talk about. It's not a secret, but I just think that this is our time to talk. Is that alright with you, Jake?"

There was a long pause before Jake said, "No one ever asked me before, I mean, what did I think? I never did much talking anyway when I was around old people. I'm just a boy. Everybody says I'm supposed to listen except to answer the questions when an adult asks. I like just being able to talk with you this way but, Mister Dewey, you're the first person ever let me. The way I thought, my mama, my teachers, they were pushing food and facts in me 'til I'd either explode or get smart. You're asking me what I think like I was already some smart person."

"Well, Jake I believe that smart is not a matter of quality, as much as a matter of quantity. If we've got a mind, old or young, we have the quality of what people call smart. The difference in people is what quantity of smart—why don't we use the word intelligence—that they are able to put together for themselves. It is my belief that you are already smart. Maybe what I can do is help you to fill out that quantity, what the capacity of your mind can be nourished into being. Don't you think though, that I'm the only person working on that project. God, your mother, your teachers, and other people you will have in your life in the future, will all be working on the quantity in that mind of yours. I'm just one old man, at one particular point in time, who would like to have a go at it because I have got so much I want you to know about. Is that a worthy working arrangement?"

Jake nodded with a touch of uncertainty in his manner.

"All right," said Samuel, shifting his position for a new start. "Let's get back to what you have been doing of late."

"I like the way it sounds when you put it out there, Mister Dewey. Do you think I can do it?"

"I'm counting on you right from the beginning, Jake."

Jake described his day at school, the subjects that had been under review. Samuel was getting an understanding about the pace of Jake's education so he would not go too far beyond the curriculum into areas that would be so foreign to Jake that he would be frustrated, unable to relate out of his already acquired knowledge. Samuel intended to keep in step while easing the boy into a higher level of confidence in using his knowledge as an interactive ability. Jake had put it right. At this time in his life it seemed parent and teachers were "stuffing" facts in as hard as they could. The part Samuel sought to play was to show the lad how to digest that input into some kind of meaningful knowledge. Samuel could give him some life skills through the telling of his life experiences, but he could not appear to be just "stuffing" him further.

"Sometimes, Mister Dewey, we get really silly when I am with my friends. Today we were teasing each other and I made up a rhyme about my friend Willie's name.

'Willie Womble swallowed a marble.

When Willie coughed it up

Did Willie's marble Womble?'"

Samuel laughed with genuine enthusiasm.

"But see, Mister Dewey, Willie did not think it was very funny. He thought I was making fun of him. I think if he could have thought of a rhyme using my name, he would have made it a game. When he couldn't, it was not a game and he was a target. It hurt him and made him mad at the same time and all at once he wasn't my friend. That wasn't what I wanted."

Samuel nodded, slowly, his lips pursed. "Sometimes, Jake, when we are having a good day or something has made us feel really full of ourselves, we get 'carried away.' That can happen to boys and old men. We get to racing along with the circumstances—a beautiful day, a good grade, an act of kindness, and I think we forget our sensitivity capacity. We all have a sensitivity capacity. Have you ever thought about yours?"

"No sir. I've never thought about what I didn't know I had."

Samuel smiled, chuckled. "Oh, you have it. You just told me about it. You said your rhyme hurt your friend and that wasn't what you wanted. What you meant was you didn't intend to hurt your friend or damage the bond that made him your friend. When I used to do something like that I would say to myself, oh, it's okay. I was just 'funning.' That wasn't always enough.

"After you were here last I thought more about our conversation about the loss we each had with the early deaths of our fathers. That started me thinking about my grandfather and how he tried to be a kind of substitute for my father. Then today you tell me about teasing your friend about the alliteration in his name and I laughed so hard because my grandpa's first name, as I told you, was Benoni and my grandma's name was Sabrah. Now just how much do you think you could use those names in rhyme?" He chuckled again. "And they each had last names that seemed to be unassociated with their first: Benoni Dewey and Sabrah Worthington. Don't you know they spent their lives with someone making up rhymes with those names! So don't be so upset about what you did. It was innocent. You didn't mean to hurt the feelings of your friend and if he took it that way, well, he has a problem. Of course it wouldn't hurt to be extra considerate of Willie for a few days." Samuel turned away, picked something up and turned back to Jake, holding it up for him to see.

"I got out this very heavy hammer to show you. I told you my grandpa was a blacksmith and this is one of the hammers he used in the blacksmith shop he had, first in Springfield, Massachusetts and then in Hanover, New Hampshire. Pick it up," he encouraged the boy.

Jake reached casually over to pick it up and the hammer almost pulled him down. "Oh, that's heavy!"

Samuel's chest quaked in a chortle. "It is heavy because he had to use it to do heavy work. One of the vivid things that I remember about my grandpa was that he was very strong. He could swing that hammer down on a piece of iron with such force that sparks would fly in all directions. It fascinated me to watch him at work because all his actions seemed to be cause and effect. He would bang down the hammer and sparks flew. He would bang at another bar and the iron would begin to bend into some desired shape. He would put the piece back in the fire and it would turn red again. It seemed that every action he took in the blacksmith's shop produced a responsive action. He could mold and make things and they were things that were useful. He did it all with the strength of his own body. I could watch all day when he let me. Finally he began putting me to use. 'Bring me that bar, or that hammer, or those long-handled tongs' he would call, and I would scurry to accommodate. I thought that the more I was useful, the more time he would let me stand and watch.

"Now, that old hammer is all I have to remind me of those days of my youth with Benoni the blacksmith. That hammer just sits. The only use it gets now is occasionally to crack a walnut. It's still good for that. Benoni Dewey, however, was more than just a blacksmith."

Jake was intently listening to Samuel. He could visualize the fire in that blacksmith's forge. He thought he could even see Benoni swinging the hammer. In his mind Benoni looked a lot like Samuel, only with big muscles that popped out of his shirt when he would bang down that hammer.

Samuel didn't rush his story. He could see that Jake was engrossed so he gave him processing time.

"How did he have time to do other things, Mister Dewey? I bet people found all kinds of things for him to do for them. I have been to the blacksmith shop of Mister Morris near the river and he has so much to do he has four hands at work with him all day long."

"You're right, Jake. Benoni had plenty of work in Hanover, but one day he had unexpected good luck and it changed the style of his life. He won the lottery! He won five hundred dollars in a lottery."

Samuel never tried to assume that Jake didn't understand a term. That too would be treating him like an adult might treat a child. Instead, if he suspected a term might be unknown to Jake, or at least somewhat strange, he would fill in more information as a qualification. Fortunately, Jake's face was a true mirror of his mind. With a little conscious animation that Samuel tried to mix in with his stories, along with extra information, most of the time Samuel could just talk on and spin his tale. Jake liked that as well because he quickly had become adjusted to the pitch and flow of Samuel's words and he was able to understand the old man in a way he had never been able to understand another adult.

"Yes, he had bought three tickets in a local lottery for fifty cents each. He had not let Sabrah know because she would not want him to engage in such a game of chance. Sabrah's father, Samuel Worthington," Samuel tapped his chest, "I was named for him, was part of an old Massachusetts family whose ancestor had fought in England under Cromwell in the Civil War. He was a Puritan—very intense and strict in his religious beliefs. That family still held to those same beliefs, which discouraged gambling.

"Benoni was overjoyed with his good fortune but he had to tell his wife in such a way that she would suppress her inclination at judgment and see his winning as an opportunity for all the family. He rushed home and through the front door making as much noise as he possibly could, found Sabrah, picked her up and swung her wide. 'My dear, at last we prosper! God has blessed us.' As he explained what had happened, he didn't hold back anything, and he hoped he saw his wife's face grow from suspicion to celebration.

"Benoni no longer wanted to remain just a blacksmith. He had never said that to his family, but now he could. He decided as he looked around Hanover that he saw other possibilities. Dartmouth College, that Eleazar Wheelock had started in seventeen seventy-three, was a solid foundation for the town. In eighteen-oh-two, Benoni had already leased the Tavern that General Ebenezer Brewster had built on the other side of town and had turned it into *Dewey's Coffee Shop*. Sabrah would not tolerate his operating a tavern. His small home at Thirty-eight College Street was not adequate for his family so, with those winnings, in eighteen-oh-nine, he built a fine new two-story house into which he moved his family and coffee house. He continued to operate as a blacksmith and it is, of course, there that I observed him at work at his forge.

"My grandfather also was active as a member of the local Congregational Church and was referred to in public as 'Deacon'. After my father died, my mother took me with my brother and sisters to spend long periods, mostly in the summer, in Hanover with her parents. I remember that about this time there was a public drama over the ownership of Dartmouth College.

"The State of New Hampshire held that the original charter from seventeen sixty-nine was invalid, and the Legislature set up a separate governing body and changed the college to Dartmouth University. The original charter had been issued by King George the Third, and it was operated as a private college associated with the Congregational Church. That case was argued right up to the United States Supreme Court, which ruled that the charter was in fact valid. As part of the vigorous local debate, Benoni, along with James Weelock and Benjamin Gilbert, were chosen as a committee to define the position of the church in the controversy. They wrote a long paper narrating the origins and progression of the church difficulties in connection with the Dartmouth case, and they supported the position of the college.

"He also was active in town matters and many times a town meeting was held at his house. He was concerned about the local schools outside the college. His youngest daughter, Temperance, was just eight years older than I, so he thought of education in terms of his children and his grandchildren. When the town voted to build a new school, he was placed on the five- man committee to carry out the task. I think, Jake, that it was through the example of my grandpa Dewey that I took an interest in so many things in my life.

"After I had gone away, Grandpa turned over Dewey's Coffee House to one of his sons, William. Everybody called him 'Corset Bill' because, while Grandpa was big and strong, his son was big and fat. He was known to wear corsets and people considered him vain. Under the strong influence of his mother, he fought against drinking and the coffee house became a temperance house, and the pious were never big spenders."

"Benoni must have been a very smart man. I didn't hear you say he went to college," Jake said, curiosity his expression.

"No. You're right. He didn't have a lot of formal education but he liked to read and he liked to listen. Any blacksmith's forge is a place of action as well as a place to talk and listen. Sooner or later everybody came there and most just blended into whatever might be the current topic of conversation."

"Ain't that the truth? Any time I go by Mister Morris's I like to stop as long as I can to listen. I dare not join in the conversation because I'm just a boy, but," Jake looked down in humility, then brightened, "I can listen."

After Jake left for home, Samuel continued to think about Benoni and Sabrah and the influence they had on his youth. His grandparents were not inclined to sit him down and tell him long stories about events in their lives. With them, he had watched their lives unfold. It was fortuitous that such people were available early in his life who could provide positive influences for his adolescence. He had been fortunate, surrounded by so much that was stable.

Jake did not have that stability. He was getting a good enough education and he was an inquisitive boy. A rooming house, however, was not a good setting for a boy to find role models. And Jake's mother, Myna Cooper, seemed overwhelmed with her function as a mother. Her actions betrayed her feeling of inadequacy. Samuel observed that she gave what attention she could to her children in reverse order of age, the most to the youngest and the least going to Jake. For him she had expectations.

I can't give to Jake what Benoni gave to me and I am in no position to try, he thought. My stories can only supply for him more insight on which to make his model. I've started out as if I were giving him my life story. That may have been natural but I'm not the story. If I am, I'm trying to be his Benoni. Get back to the way you started, Samuel. Let Jake find what interests him in your 'house of treasures.' Let that be his inspiration, not your story. He finds the interest, then you expand the interest by a tale from your experience. Of course it will come from your experience but it will be Jake who found the key to open the door. This will not be simple but it is the only way to proceed unless it all becomes self-centered in you. Honestly, he mused, this really came from my need for relevance. Don't be despondent. You'll satisfy your relevance in the process anyway. The test will be if you can succeed in providing relevance for Jake. He's the test.

So Samuel felt reset. He settled in his favorite chair beside his artifacts piled up on the table, and mused over what he had learned in his lifetime of experiences. In the end, he reflected, the thing old people have is self. Their active life is gone, their profession, most of their friends, the things that had consumed their days. Life just tolerates them unless they find something on which to concentrate beyond themselves. The paradox is that we have to reach outside ourselves to find the inspiration that consumes us. We cannot do it from the inside. If we are lucky we have spent all our lives discovering, inventing for ourselves, this skill we call life. Pouring himself a cup of strong coffee, he considered his gains in knowledge and wisdom.

I have spent a lifetime discovering new interests, new people, new opportunities beyond myself that have lit a fire in me, he thought. Late in life my body limits my inspiration. I have to find a substitute for that *modus operandi*. Jake may be for me the inspiration for my resuscitation. I have to go out beyond myself and make my relevance in him, in his need, in order to find my own salvation. Yes, Jake and I have much to give to each other.

Chapter Three

Wiggly Grit

"I been wondering about something I picked up over there the other day that felt like a wiggly rock, Mister Dewey. I know I have never seen a rock that could bend. A rock is always hard—hard as a rock." Jake pointed to a low case of four shelves with glass doors. "It's over there in that case."

"Get it out, boy, and let's take a look at it," suggested Samuel. Jake obliged. "That case, from which you chose this rock, is my sample collection of minerals and rocks from North Carolina. We called them 'specimens.' I guess my interest in rocks and minerals started as early as when I watched Benoni hammer on that iron and turn it into something useful. Then in my young adult days I went to sea and traveled almost everywhere in the world and saw many amazing things from precious gems to meteorites. My interest grew and I began acquiring my collection of specimens. I didn't know what I would do with this growing collection, but I was drawn to have an example of each thing that I could touch—an example of my own.

"In those first forty years of my life I also was very successful in business and so in eighteen forty-five, I retired to work on projects that appealed just to me. It sounds selfish as I speak of it now, but my life became so much more inspired and I became an amateur mineralogist and geologist. Around the world people trained in those fields were making startling discoveries and I sought a place among them. I had some formal college training but I already had considerable experience gained in the field. My name was attached to a good reputation."

As Samuel spoke, Jake held the wiggly rock carefully in his hand.

"I established an office in New York and then became interested in large tracts of land in the southern states that were being marketed as rich with minerals and important geological deposits. I made trips to Virginia and made valuable contacts in Richmond, the capital, where there was public interest in mineral land. Many large acreage tracts were deeded after the Revolutionary War to speculators who hoped to become rich selling farms or mining the minerals that might be under the ground. It was common for men like George Washington, Patrick Henry, and Aaron Burr to become so involved in this speculation on the unlimited richness they all saw in America, that they were willing to risk their fortunes and their reputations. One such man was Timothy Pickering, who was Secretary of State under Presidents Washington and Adams. Among his attempts at speculation, he bought a large acreage in Stokes County in North Carolina from a Moravian lawyer named Gottlieb Schober.

"When I was in Richmond I heard talk about the marvelous mineral resources of this land and of a range of mountains named for the Saura Indians. I was interested, so I made a trip to North Carolina to look at this mineral-rich land. I was struck immediately by the possibilities of what was called the Northern Piedmont. Right in the middle of Stokes County, in that Piedmont, there was a small range of dramatic-looking mountains. I know of nowhere else in the country that there is such a range all within a single county. The Dan River, which is an upper extension of the Roanoke River watershed, originated just to the north in Virginia and swung down into North Carolina diagonally across the county from northwest to southeast. The river cut right through those Sauratown Mountains. On my first exploration I had the impression that this area appeared to be like a miniature laboratory for the concentrated examination of minerals and geological forms. There were such an extensive number of minerals and geological formations present. Right away I was attracted by what I believed to be unique conditions and by the particularly interesting people who lived in what one might expect to be a remote and ordinary neighborhood.

"Stokes County had been partitioned about five years earlier and the center of the new county, which in North Carolina was usually sought for locating the county courthouse, was found to be in the middle of the Sauratown Mountain range just beside the flowing Dan River. It was a picturesque spot but almost nobody lived there. So a town was surveyed, divided into lots, and a nice knoll was chosen on which to build the new brick courthouse. A courthouse always drew a community of professional men and those who had business with the court. Each quarter there would be a session of court held for about a week. The judges and all the lawyers, whose business depended on the cases to be heard that week, and all the people who originated those cases, would come to town and the population would increase several times. So in addition to the houses, there were soon two hotels at the courthouse. This new village was first named Crawford, in honor of a politician of national note, but some citizens didn't like the man, so they changed the name of the town to Danbury.

"I came down to Danbury from Lynchburg, Virginia and found good accommodations at the McCandless Hotel on the courthouse square—where I also took my meals. Back in that time I was a pretty vigorous man and took the opportunity, even at my first meal, to begin to introduce myself. I was referred immediately to the local doctor, John Pepper, whose home was just south of town over Three Sisters Mountain at Flat Shoals Creek.

"I rode over there that day and found the good doctor puttering in his garden. Doctor John Pepper was a very spry, bearded gentleman, about a decade older than I, who had come to Stokes County from Christiansburg, Virginia about twenty-five years earlier. He had received his medical training at Transylvania College in Lexington, Kentucky, and during his medical studies, took a wide-ranging interest beyond medical science.

"Straight away I found him to meet admirably my continuously sought standard as a man of inquiring mind. We sat in the breeze-way between the two sections of his log house. After some pleasantries, mostly concerning the pastoral beauty of the location, I identified the reason I was in town.

"Doctor Pepper," I began, "I fashion myself to be a geologist and mineralogist, not by academic training but by the more practical academy known as experience. I went to sea as a very young man and traveled much of the world, visiting most of the principal ports of Europe, South America, and the East Indies. I retired after nearly twenty-five years in the merchant service and organized my own business as a ship-broker in New York City. I traded throughout the South, the West Indies and much of South America and after ten years I sold that business. In the course of both those adventures, and I call them adventures advisedly, I developed an unsuspected attraction to the range of the world's mineral deposits and the field of geology in general. So when I left my brokerage business, I did so in order to enter more directly into the two fields I had gravitated to as my avocation: geology and politics. I sought you out in order to discuss the former, although we may entertain ourselves on the latter at another time.

"Doctor Pepper was anxious to say that geology and politics similarly attracted much of the time he had outside his medical practice. We confirmed our mutual enthusiasm with some fine cold cider as we rocked. It was on this day that the doctor introduced me first to the rock you hold in your hand. He said to me, 'it is itacolumite, and around here it is referred to commonly as *'wiggly grit.'*

"You see, Jake, you very naturally called it what the people there in Stokes County called it: wiggly.

"Doctor Pepper went on to tell me that the stone was an example of flexible sandstone and it was found in the Sauratown, particularly in an area around Quaker Gap. Then he added a teaser, testing my reaction like an angler seeks the bite of a fish, by saying, 'In several places in the world it is typically connected with the discovery of diamonds.'"

Jake was now using both hands to gently twist the rock in his hands. Even in this dark interior, the flecks of mica gave off a faint sparkle. "Make your own test, Jake. You can bend it, then set it here on my desk and you will see it slowly bend back to its original shape." Samuel watched as the boy studied the rock reset into its natural form.

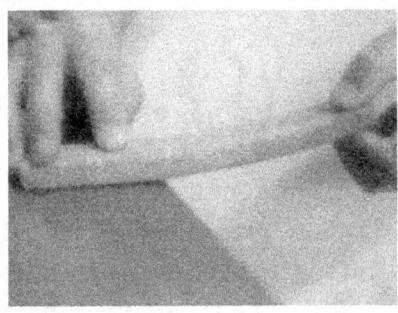

Intacolumite

"How can a rock bend, Mister Dewey, and then bend back on its own?"

"As Doctor Pepper put it that day at the cabin and on many other occasions when he visited in Danbury, at first it was thought that it was caused by slabs or scales of mica observable in the rock that permitted a motion between the adjacent grains of quartz. More study then preferred to explain that it was the porous nature of the rock and the interlocking junctions between the sand grains that produce the effect. I came to believe that the ideas were interconnected because I found that after a period of drying there was less flexibility and it was clear that the mica scales created a sliding effect and an interlocking that prevented the rock from just falling apart.

"Doctor Pepper told me that this rock formation that made up the mountains that surrounded Danbury was quartzite, which is itself a hard metamorphic rock that makes up much of the surface of the earth. Quartzite is what is seen when a person looks today at the Sauratown Mountains. It is sandstone that through a changing of form, metamorphic, meaning heat and pressure, was transformed into quartzite. The Sauratown Mountains were formed when the earth's surface, exposed to horizontal pressure, friction and distortion, was pushed up, exposing that surface above the land surface surrounding it."

Samuel was pleased to note Jake's curiosity about the "wiggly rock" and the formation of quartzite. Even so, he realized it was evident that his running discourse had probably exceeded Jake's background of knowledge. If the boy were going to continue to follow the story, Samuel decided that he would need to translate some of those terms to match Jake's understanding. Otherwise, it might be too ponderous to try to explain the formation of the earth's surface. With such an effort in mind, he began with the surface in place. "Jake, it's like a crack came in the surface of the earth and one side of land pushed under the other and thrust it up higher. Can you picture that as happening millions of years ago?

"I can picture it happening like maybe an earthquake but I never saw that either."

"Well that still captures the idea. That is how to describe the rock in the higher elevations of those mountains, but in the lower levels the quartz was mixed with other metamorphic rock referred to as gneiss."

Jake looked quizzical. "Nice?"

Samuel chuckled. "It's spelled g, n, e, i, double s. But the g is soft, so yes, it's pronounced like nice." He patted the boy on the head. "Or sometimes it is referred to as 'nais' or 'schist.'" Samuel explained further. "Quartz gneiss is formed originally from molten, hot melted rock or from a mixture of minerals and organics that settled as sedimentary. Quartz schist is rock notable for the presence of layered levels of minerals in the quartz. This then returns us to that description of the make-up of itacolumite: quartz and mica." He paused. "I hope I'm not confusing you with all these terms."

"No, sir. I can keep up with you."

"Then I'll go on with my lesson. In many other places in the Sauratown, I found garnet schist, whole hillsides where small garnet could be popped out of the sandstone by the handful. Garnet is a mineral. Let me see that box over there," Dewey said, pointing Jake toward a box in the edge of the little storage space.

As Jake pulled it out he said, "It has 'Stokes' written on the top."

"Quite so, yes—I have many of the minerals that I collected in Stokes County on my shelves with my general collections. These are more, and I believe I have some garnet schist in here." He rummaged in the container and pulled out lazulite, pyrolusite, granular calcite, serpentine, anthracite, sulphur, hematite, chalcedony, hornstone, phlogopite, agate, amethist, jasper, rock crystal, copper, graphite, tourmaline, muscovite, and limonite, each marked with name and location. Then he lifted out a rock about the size of the itacolumite sample. It had the same color but looked more like a large potato with eyes stuck out all over it. Samuel worked one loose with a knife blade from his table and held it in his hand.

"That's garnet, Jake. It looks dark, almost black, but if you look closely, you will see it is red in the light. Garnet is attractive as a gem stone but these are all too small to be used as gems. Garnets also are used as an abrasive because the stone is quite hard. Larger garnet is often ground and used in various degrees of fineness to make sandpaper. You could pick out a quantity of these stones and grind them for the same purpose.

"Scattered about the yard of Doctor Pepper's house at Danbury were examples of all types of rocks and minerals that he had picked up as samples over the years. We spent hours, just as you and I are doing, Jake, picking up one formation after another, identifying it, qualifying its presence in the mountains and its abundance, and projecting the various uses to which it could be put. His yard was a virtual geological storehouse. He knew instinctively the varying rock formations and he studied to the extent that information was available to him, but he relished our conversations as a confirmation of everything he had perceived as the potential for this geological abundance."

Once into the examination of this collection of Stokes County minerals, Samuel and Jake were like prospectors, finding one item after another at which to marvel. So much new information was pouring out upon the boy that he commented he had a sensation of being stuffed. "I'll no doubt stay awake tonight trying to process all the new things you're telling me," he added. Samuel chuckled, realizing Jake was likely to do just that, and he must give the boy time to grasp the new information.

Two days later they were still on the subject of the Sauratown Mountains. "Doctor Pepper introduced me," said Samuel, "to some of his friends who shared his interest in the mineral resources and their potential commercial uses. Captain Alexander Moody and his brother, Nathaniel, already owned and operated an iron works on the river at Danbury called Moody's Tunnel Iron Works. I don't think I said before that the only thing around this site where they chose to locate their courthouse was an operating iron works. When I first came to Stokes County I found that deposits of iron ore, exposed in the natural process of erosion, were common and for about eighty years there had been furnaces to process that ore.

Even at the time of the American Revolution the state of North Carolina encouraged the production of iron with bounties of unclaimed land that was hard to cultivate. The iron furnaces could use the trees on this bounty land for charcoal which was necessary to the iron making process. It was by that time very easy to see that timber was in great demand in Stokes because huge swaths of land were denuded of trees, and combined with pastures and areas under cultivation; the whole county seemed one open vista with this line of mountains rising across the middle.

"Iron was processed in bloomeries, or furnaces, and forges for further processing were attached to either type of structure. The bloomery was simpler and usually smaller and consisted of a pit or a chimney made of earth, clay, or stone. At the bottom, a clay or metal pipe inserted in the walls allowed a natural draft, or a bellows was employed to force air into the furnace.

"Charcoal was prepared by heating timber in fire stacks to produce a nearly pure carbon fuel. One of the other common sights in Stokes was to see across the landscape these piles of wood smoking day and night being prepared for the furnaces.

"More common, as the industry grew, were furnaces that made use of the Catalan process. The Moody Furnace at Danbury, by the time I saw it, was such a Catalan furnace. Unlike the bloomery, these furnaces used water and water power so they were built near creeks or rivers.

"At Danbury, the Dan was still a small river with a fairly swift current and the flow crossed north of town and on the east side made a sharp loop. The furnace was located on the inside of that curve and a wooden dam was built across the river upstream where the loop began. The furnace was constructed of stone blocks with four sides rising about twenty-five feet. In the front, a short distance above the hearth, was an opening where a nozzle attached to a leather bellows carried pumped air into the furnace. The hearth was filled to the level of the nozzle with charcoal. On top of this layer, charcoal and iron ore were laid in separate stacks, the ore toward the back and the charcoal and limestone to the front. A blast of air from the bellows caused the burning charcoal to give off carbon monoxide gas which combined with oxygen in the ore, reducing it to a molten iron.

"At the Danbury furnace a tunnel from the dammed river could divert a flow to the furnace to power the bellows. The lump of iron could be removed from the furnace, and water power was also used to drive a hammer that beat the iron to get out the remaining impurities, then beat it into the form of a bar which was marketed to blacksmiths. Molten iron could also be bled off, and the overflow could be diverted directly to the attached forge and foundry where it poured into forms, or ingots, to be worked by heat and hammer into tools, utensils, or weapons as required.

"Edward and Gideon Moore operated a furnace up on Double Creek. The Moody brothers had bought up many of the early ironworks furnaces as well as their bounty grants and now owned more than seven thousand acres. There were furnaces on Neatman Creek and Snow Creek, so iron mining and manufacturing appeared to represent a strong future industrial base for Stokes County.

Moody's Tunnel Iron Works - Danbury, NC

"My conversations with Doctor Pepper and his friends convinced me, and I soon persuaded them that distribution of their iron products or ingots could not depend on the small batteaux that carried farm products on the Dan River. The river was too shallow in Stokes County and those boats were not made to carry a heavy product. Some iron could be distributed regionally in wagons, but the roads were badly maintained and often not dependable for transport. The ideal method of transportation for any mining activity was the railroad—that was rapidly being built into a system.

"This was the kind of prototype that I saw present throughout the American South. Dependent on farming practices that needed an abundance of labor, the Southern planters found themselves trapped in the abominable practice of human slavery. It was the potential of the exploitation of the mining and mineral resources in the South that could liberate the region from the dependence on slavery.

"When I would sit in conversation with Doctor Pepper, the Moody brothers, Reuben Golding, the Moore's, Winston Fulton or James Davis, I was talking to men who were not large slave holders, because their hilly land could never yield the size of cotton and tobacco crops of the Deep South. Still, they were so imbued with the dependence on slavery as a Southern necessity that they saw slave labor as the only means of labor for mining and manufacturing. 'That is not true,' I would say to them. It is not necessary that you use slavery only because it exists. In manufacturing, you will be able to pay an honest wage without the ownership of labor. You can free yourselves from the curse that holds you back competitively with the North and debilitates your society.

"Jake, I had traveled the world, and in the process I had seen many countries where slavery was a common practice, not just the American southern states. I never saw anything good about slavery. Wherever I came in contact with slavery, people placed less value on life and their moral values were shallow. I found it difficult to make a true friendship with a person who willingly owned slaves. So as I determined to attach my future vocation to the Southern economy, I also had to recognize I would be an advocate of the abolition of slavery. It was an uneasy course. Even these men in Danbury, who wished to exploit the opportunity to make profitable investments in manufacturing, were reluctant to give up slavery as a condition even when it no longer served their best interests.

"They showed me abundant deposits of alum, a whole cliff that was above an alum spring owned by Doctor Pepper. We looked at coal deposits in the southern part of Stokes and a fine grade of clay for making brick and pipe. Mica deposits were concentrated enough for what looked like inexhaustible mining. Reuben Golding and a few others incorporated the Stokes Iron Mining Company, for the purpose of exploring for copper, lead, gold, iron and other materials or minerals. Through my North Carolina friends I was referred to men in Texas and Tennessee who had been weaned on the mineral marvels of Stokes County and who were now gathering such specimens of minerals and rocks to be found in the vicinity of their new homes.

"I became the agent for these men, and speculators like them throughout the South, with the money and stock markets of the East. I was offering large tracts of land for sale as well as mineral rights. In

North Carolina and Virginia I became directly involved in the chartering of a railroad from High Point or Salem, North Carolina to Lynchburg, Virginia, to run through Danbury. This meant that I had to obtain the approval of both state legislatures for an acceptable negotiated charter for the railroad. I learned very quickly the difficulty of negotiating inter-state charters for any commercial project.

"These two states had for years attempted to expand commerce on the Roanoke River, which wound back and forth between the two, and eventually emptied into the Atlantic in North Carolina. This was one of the early projects in which George Washington and Patrick Henry had been stockholders. The states would alternately support and reject the terms of operating the navigation system. Only in brief windows of opportunity was there enough cooperation to improve the river course to accommodate commercial transport. The states were still in only moderate co-operation when I approached each legislature in turn to charter our railroad.

"I succeeded in gaining a charter in North Carolina as the High Point, Salem, Germantown and Virginia Railroad, but it was only one of a number of proposed routes for which charters were requested. Within a month bills had been introduced in the same legislature for the Piedmont Range Railroad, Manufacturing and Mineral Company and the Salem and Germantown Railroad. All these charters could not be successful, so the competition between them became fierce. I already had established my land office in Richmond so I thought that I had support at the highest level for my charter. I was defeated by two factors that I perhaps should have anticipated. First, the delegate from Lynchburg was lobbied heavily by a competing charter and was lukewarm to ours, though he did not speak against it. Then several influential North Carolinians appeared in Richmond and boldly put it about that the High Point Railroad Charter was nothing but a 'humbug' and it would be repealed by the next North Carolina legislature.

"I was not discouraged even though I had spent more than a thousand dollars in the project already. I kept up my efforts politically but at the expense of land sales. I suggested that the railroad be built from High Point to Danbury but no one was prepared to speculate to that extent.

"Eventually it was the Civil War, fought over that curse of slavery, that ended all these enthusiastic efforts at mineral exploitation and railroad building. It is ironic, Jake, but on the last day of that horrible war, April nine, eighteen sixty-five, the day General Lee surrendered to General Grant, that the Yankee General Stoneman and his western army had rendezvoused in Danbury. His men were in the process of blowing up the Iron Works which had been making rebel cannon balls."

"Was that the end of all your work with Doctor Pepper?"

Samuel sighed as if in apology. "Yes, Jake, I'm afraid it was. By the end of that war Doctor Pepper and all his friends were like their counterparts throughout the South. They lost half their wealth when their slaves were freed: all their money, and any stock they had in investments were worthless. One thing did surprisingly survive and has prospered ever since. I told you about those cliffs of sulfur. Well there were many springs throughout the Sauratown Mountains and some came out through those sulfur deposits. The taste of the sulfur in the water was not particularly pleasant but it was considered to be healthful and people began to come by train and stage to Stokes where three summer hotels were built at Piedmont Springs, Moore's Springs, and Vade Mecum.

"Families would spend weeks at a time at one of the springs," Samuel made air quotes with his fingers, "'for their health.' It was healthy for them and it helped cushion the disappointment of the losses of the war. I came back to Stokes County on several occasions and spent time at Piedmont Springs just above Danbury. The freestone spring water that came out of the hill there just beside the sulfur spring was used to pipe water into Danbury. Doctor Pepper himself attempted to open his sulfur spring to tourists, as a marvel of nature, but it never turned enough profit for him to build a hotel.

"It is sometimes very sad, Jake, that people's lives can become so altered by outside events. I often think of Doctor Pepper who has now been dead for many years. He was a country visionary and Danbury was an intellectual island in a sea of mediocrity. Had Doctor Pepper succeeded in any of his pursuits, that island might have been transformed."

One of Samuel W. Dewey's letters to Dr. John Pepper, 1858

Chapter Four

A Thirteen-year-old Midshipman

"Do you know what that is?" asked Samuel as Jake twirled what looked like a handle of some sort. "That is a treasure from my very earliest days."

"Looks to me like it punches holes in something," Jake said in a questioning tone. He thrust his hand in a stabbing motion. "You got two of them I saw back there."

"I once had four or five but I've used them for other things over the years."

Jake waited for the explanation that usually came at this point but Samuel had fallen into one of his reveries. The boy waited patiently because these pauses, he had come to believe, made for a better story and Samuel never paused long.

"That, Jake, is a belaying pin used on a sailing ship to secure lines of rigging. It was inserted in a wooden pinrail so that the ropes could be wound round. When I was thirteen years old, my mother and my siblings were living in Boston, as I told you. My father had been dead for about seven years and as we children got older it was more and more difficult for Mother to work to support us and to watch over us at the same time. She had not remarried, as many women in those days quickly did after the death of their husbands. Two could manage the children more effectively than one, was the prevailing logic. She received a pension of twenty dollars a month as the widow of a sailor who died in war, which helped her particularly because it was a dependable income.

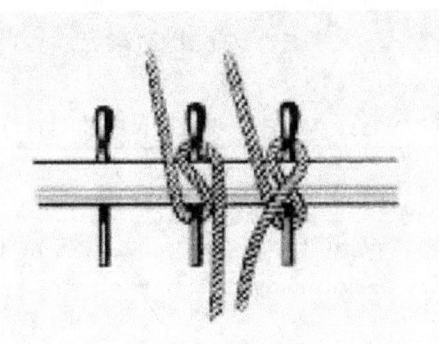

Belaying Pin

"As the oldest child I was expected to help her care for the others, and I must admit I was not good at that. Mother was constantly scolding me when one of my siblings got into trouble or hurt themselves and that made me feel guilty and angry at the same time.

"Boston was of course a sailing town, and my father had been a sailor, so I was always exposed to the adventure, and the dangers, of the sea. I talked to my grandfather Benoni first about my problems with my role in the family. You remember Benoni who lived in New Hampshire. My first thought was that my mother might agree to take me and the others to live with him. I knew that would be a hardship on everyone. That's when the idea came to me that without me there would not be so many mouths to feed, so I told my grandfather I wanted to go to sea, to become a sailor. He didn't seem surprised. I'm sure he had observed my unhappiness. He only agreed that he would support my request if my mother came to him for advice.

"My mother did not agree. At first she dismissed the idea out of hand. Then two of the families for which she did laundry moved away within two months and she had no success in replacing that income. After that she herself took sick and she saw what misery I had in trying to do all the housework. I wanted to help her but I didn't want that kind of responsibility. It took several months but finally she gave her consent for me to become a sailor. I was thirteen.

"I really don't know how much it influenced her decision, but a good friend of my father's, Captain Ashman, agreed to take me on as a 'midshipman ordinary' on the brig, *Guilford,* bound for the East Indies.

We sailed out of Boston on March fifteen, eighteen twenty, and returned the middle of January, eighteen twenty-one; I don't remember the day."

Jake was staring at Samuel with his mouth slightly ajar. There was a strange mix of disbelief, awe, and jealousy in his eyes. Samuel smiled to himself, observing the boy who was holding the cylindrical end of the belaying pin in his right hand and pounding the handle softly into his left palm. An unconscious body action that left his mind free to accelerate in mystery, Samuel surmised. Young Jake is eleven and this man before him had gone to sea at nearly the same age.

"You were really just thirteen?" Jake said, his tone belying an unwillingness to accept the fact without further corroboration. "Weren't you scared?"

"Jake, as I look back on it now, I was so happy to have finally been permitted to go that fear had to wait. My mother cried just as she had that day they told her my father had died. I was thankful that Grandfather Benoni was there to comfort her because I don't believe I could have left her so unhappy.

"Captain Ashman put me right to work and, when I was not occupied with a task, I was by his side and he was the constant teacher. He understood that on such a long trip I was going to get homesick, but if he could keep me busy, he would ease some of that pain. I was enthusiastic but my lack of knowledge was prodigious.

"Jeremiah Underwood had been warrant officer under Captain Ashman on previous sailings and he had been promoted to midshipman. We held the same rank but it was obvious from the start of the voyage that Jeremiah functioned as the true midshipman on the *Guilford*. Jeremiah was just two years older than I and we developed strong bonds of friendship in spite of the fact that he was a much more experienced sailor. There were four other boys on the ship. Two of them had run away from home and had lived on the street in Boston. The other two were farm boys and they had not even had the benefit of being near the sea as they grew up. It may seem unusual to you, but back then many a homeless or wayward boy became a sailor by the time he was thirteen."

Jake bunched his eyebrows with a quizzical frown. "What if you got out there and found out you hated being a sailor, or the sea made you sick, or the captain or his men were mean to you. What would you have done then?"

"I guess I didn't think through all those possibilities because I wanted so to get away from my life at home. Anyway, even if I had, once the *Guilford* left port such questions as those were of no use. I found out right away that in life, Jake, you make choices and then you have to live with the results."

"I know about that, but you made such a big choice. You could have died at sea, a long way from home. I ain't afraid to make choices as long as I don't make bad ones." Jake shook his head, blew air and appeared incredulous as he stared at his mentor. "I can't believe you could have made such a choice as a boy."

"Jake, I'm not trying to preach to you but if you are afraid to make the big choices in life, sometimes you may miss the biggest opportunities to accomplish great things. I don't mean you should take unnecessary chances or stupid risks. Choices should be made with a sober mind and with a consideration for others. Your choices affect not only you but others who care for you. My choice had a devastating effect on my mother. I knew it would. But I knew I was more of a burden than a help and I convinced myself that she would be better off if she did not have to worry about me. I said I convinced myself because I came to know that I did not make that choice really thinking about her wishes. I convinced myself. I got better later in life about making choices that considered me as well as those around me." As he spoke to Jake, Samuel suddenly realized that the boy might go home and tell his mother that he had suggested that he run away to sea. He recognized that young people hear these stories, but they translate them into their own time and place and some translate better than others.

"We sailed south along the Atlantic coast. The *Guilford* was a two-masted, square rigged Brig with a gaff sail rigged to her aft mast. She was a hundred ten feet long, had a thirty-two foot beam, and weighed four hundred seventy-five tons and had been built at the end of the war at Newburyport on the Merrimac by Retire Becket as part of the commercial sailing fleet of Massachusetts. Jake, you are perhaps more familiar with size in terms of the number of masts you observe on a ship in the harbor, but this was a good-sized ship with a crew of twenty-two, a little larger than might usually be required on a Brig."

Jake's face lit up. "Oh, I can identify a Brig, Mister Dewey, when I see it on the Delaware even in light sail."

Brig sailing ship

"I apologize, Jake for not giving you due credit as a sailor," Dewey responded with encouragement. "When I talk about those days a long time ago, I begin to visualize myself as a boy and I think of how little I knew—how the intricacies of the ship sometimes almost overwhelmed me. Because I was the son of a sea captain, I guess I thought everything about the ship should come easily to me and, when it did not, I took it as a personal failure. Fortunately Captain Ashman sensed my concern and rarely assumed knowledge that he had not given to me himself in instruction. That helped put me more at ease, but if I forgot something he had told me, he was swift to show his displeasure when I made a mistake. My training, I guess, was a bargain we came to without words; he told me everything as I needed to know it, and I listened attentively."

"Did you know where your ship was going when you left port?"

"Yes, I did. Captain Ashman was very clear to my mother and to me that our destination was the East Indies and we would be gone for more than half a year. I knew that much, but I didn't know where the East Indies really were, and time didn't bother me at that age. Soon after we sailed, the captain rolled out his charts and showed me our route, at least to what he called our destination, but he was not certain yet about what route he might take to come home. We were going to Sumatra." With that, Samuel rummaged through some maps on a shelf and rolled out a colorful world map.

"Hold that corner there," said Samuel, directing the boy to one end of the map. "As I said earlier, we left Boston and sailed down the Atlantic coast to the West Indies where we stopped in Barbados to deliver a small quantity of iron and lumber. Our route across the Atlantic was called the Middle Passage, and then around the Cape of Good Hope to Cape Town where we were refitted with food and water for the passage across the Indian Ocean to Sumatra to a port called North Tally Pow.

"It was a wonder to me that just out of Cape Town we came to the place where the bright blue-green of the Atlantic Ocean fused with the darker shades of the Indian Ocean. On occasion the turbulence created by this phenomenon of amalgamation was the cause of many shipwrecks. Our passage was calm.

"For some time shipping fleets built in New England had been increasing their trade with India, the East Indies, and China. Great fortunes were built on that trade and New England shipbuilding was very profitable. Ships would leave Salem or Boston with iron, timber, molasses, consignments of tobacco and cotton. They would return with hemp from Luzon, coffee from Arabia, spices from Java, cotton from Bombay, salt from Cadiz, wine from Portugal, and tea and silk from China. Before the war in eighteen twelve, the Salem ships had established a very lucrative trade with Sumatra in pepper. By the time I made my first trip to Sumatra, the Salem fleet no longer had its monopoly trade with the island, but it was still the New England captains who ventured into this risky trade, and the Boston and Salem brokers who were willing to venture capital.

"A ship sailing for Sumatra might carry as much as two hundred thousand dollars in cash to purchase a full cargo of pepper. Pirates, who infested the Indian Ocean and the islands of the East Indies, were looking for such ships—to rob them of their coins if they were eastbound, or their cargo if they were returning to New England. They preferred the cash because they did not have to convert it. Crews on the American ships were lightly armed and the small crews were sometimes made up half of boys, so the pirates considered them an easy catch. Sometimes the heathens kept the ship and sometimes they burned it, but almost always they killed the crew.

"So the training on the outbound leg of the voyage was essential because by the time a ship rounded the Cape of Good Hope, the crew had to be able to function efficiently in case it came in contact with pirates. Speed of sail was the main protection if pirates were sighted. If ships were boarded, even the boys had to fight for their lives hand-to-hand. Except for a heavy storm in the Atlantic and some uneasy days of becalmed seas in the Indian Ocean, the voyage out was uneventful.

"Sumatra is of course a tropical island, with a strip of lowland along the beach and towering green mountains inland. The sea breaks over the coral reefs and arrives at shore in small ripples. Just beyond the sand beaches lie the villages. Small ports had sprung up at Bencoolen, Analaboo, Soo-Soo, Tangar, and the port we used at North Tally Pow. The port was only a point of contact if there were no cargo consigned to unload, and the friendly Malays dressed in bright colored sarongs seemed deceptively welcoming.

"Captain Ashman went ashore and dickered for a price and quantity of pepper with the local *datu*. Only after a price had been agreed to did the captain call for the crew to bring ashore a beam balance and weights to weigh the pepper. Then native boats, called *praus,* brought out the pepper in their smaller craft and it was loaded on the *Guilford*. The serpent in this paradise of commerce was the Malay natives who, it was known from unhappy experience, thought nothing of cutting the throats of the Americans and taking both the money and the pepper. Everyone in the crew was on high alert for any signs of deception.

"The *Guilford* took on all the pepper that was in port and had only about two thirds of what they wanted in terms of cargo. Captain Ashman negotiated an agreement to go with the *datu* up into a local river to a station where the farmers brought their pepper to supply his port. There they could barter for the balance. The captain knew that by making this passage up river he would be seriously weakening the command on the ship. He had not yet paid the *datu* and the pepper available in the port was all loaded on the *Guilford*. If he were to take this trip, he had to leave the ship as strongly manned as possible while he was away. It was a difficult choice. He took me and Midshipman Jeremiah Underwood aside and asked if we were willing to go with him and leave all the other men with the ship. He left it to us to decide individually. Right away we both said enthusiastically that we would go. My heart was in my throat, but I thought this was my first chance to be a man, necessary to a task.

"Three of the native boats left from the dock. The *datu* and three men were in the first boat. One of those men, a little smaller and less threatening than the others, was obviously a guide and the *datu* talked to him a long time. We thought the conversation was necessary in order to give him instructions, but during that time the smaller man seemed very agitated and unhappy with what he was being told. The captain, Jeremiah and I, along with one man to pilot the boat came second and four men followed in the last boat. We were all armed but if there was going to be any fighting we were obviously out-numbered. Captain Ashman's instructions were to keep our weapons in our belts at all times unless he fired first. We were to let him do all the talking and to try very hard to show no fear. We assumed that the *datu* intended to take the shipment of pepper peaceably, but there was no certainty.

"We were on the river for about three hours before we came to a clearing with huts and a small dock, everything surrounded in what appeared as very green, dense jungle. There were about a dozen armed men standing around the dock, four or five women and about the same number of children. Only the children showed any animation. The men did not seem hostile but impassive.

"The negotiations were made by the *datu* in a language none of us could understand. They could have been making plans to kill us and boil us for dinner. We were taken into a grass- covered hut and sat on small individual benches with three men from the village. The negotiations then included Captain Ashman, with the *datu* translating as an intermediary. The captain agreed to pay a price just higher than what he had paid for the first part of the load believing, I thought, that he needed to give something extra as good will. It was agreed that payment would be made for the full load when it was on board the *Guilford*.

"It seemed the negotiations had concluded successfully, when the native leader said something to one of his men standing near the door to the hut. He went out and brought back forcibly the little man we had concluded was the guide. He was pushed to a kneeling position. Before we could take it in, the guard took a broad sword from his belt and with one powerful swing lopped off the head of the guide. The head flew up away from the body, which crumpled twitching to the ground, spun in a wild arch across the room, and fell into my lap with a noticeable plop. I am sure I reacted with a startled expression, but even as the one exposed eye of the head winked at me, I held steady, determined not to show fear. My clothes were bloodied, but I stood and let the head roll off my body and across the floor to the body it had just left. The *datu* did not flinch at the loss of one of his men, as if he expected or understood why he had been killed. I stood, I remember, because I could feel the soaking blood and I thought if I didn't get rid of that head right then, I would pee in my pants.

"By the time we left the village we were a convoy of five boats, three of which were loaded with pepper and a single pilot. When we arrived back at the *Guilford*, we were relieved that the ship was as we had left it. The crew was startled by my bloodied uniform for which I had an incomplete explanation. Later the captain explained generally to the crew, and in greater detail to Jeremiah and me that the guide had been killed because the location to which he had taken us was secret even to the *datu*. He had betrayed his chief. Captain Ashman then added that there had been a moment when a decision was being taken whether we should all be killed to preserve the secret location. Since killing us also meant killing the *datu* and his men and would leave the natives empty-handed, they made an example of the guide. At that point," Samuel looked directly into Jake's eyes, and said with solemnity, "for the first time, I felt ill."

Jake's eyes had visibly dilated and his mouth was ajar. "He just l-lopped it off in . . . one swing?"

"Clean cut," said Samuel, with an exemplary sweep of his straightened fingers across his throat. "Except for the flying blood, it was the neatest slaughter I ever was to see—man or beast.

"Captain Ashman seemed satisfied with his negotiations in Sumatra, particularly because his crew had behaved with such maturity and discipline. A teacher works energetically for months knowing that at some point, which he may or may not control, there will be a day of testing whose results will be the ultimate measure of his success. A few men, half boys, had entered into a life or death experience and had performed perfectly as a crew — several individuals, a single instrument. A ship captain could ask for none better. They deserved to sail to China as a reward.

"It might seem that after three months at sea, the prospect of a month more of voyaging before turning for home might have been a disappointment, particularly for the younger boys. On the contrary, now they considered themselves sailors and they had mastered the ship which would take them to riches and adventure.

"The *Guilford* sailed around the south end of Sumatra through the Sunda Strait between Sumatra and Java and caught the northern currents passing between Borneo, and then the Philippines to the east on the South China Sea to Canton, the only city in China where European nations were allowed to trade. Canton was a city of wonder. All the European countries had factories in the city, even the United States. There were said to be a million people. Everyone went there to get rich. The Chinese could channel their exotic products through the port to the eager markets of the West without risking social penetration into their mainland.

"We all got our chance to spend hours on shore, amazed by the different nationalities we observed. Captain Ashman advanced some of our wages so that we could purchase items for our personal profit or for gifts for our families. I didn't know anything about spices or exotic woods or silks, for that matter. But silks were neatly packed and I could fill my own ship's trunk. So I picked some colors that I liked. Then I bought some novelties that pleased me, like those over there."

Samuel pointed to four small frames painted blue and gold, inside of which were three-dimensional scenes of Chinese towns and landscapes. Jake picked one and began to study it more closely. "Everything is so tiny — and exact. How can they make it so fine?" he wondered aloud.

"They use cork, Jake, very thin layers of cork. Then on the flat surface and using a tiny knife, they cut out the side of a house or a tree. After that they paste it on a background that they have painted with clouds, by putting one layer on another. That way they build up the scene so it appears to have real depth.

"I also got a whole set of carved wooden figures of Chinese people going about their daily lives. You know, I kept these for myself and I used to study them for hours until I could almost imagine people moving along the landscape. They kept my memories of China very vivid for me. I later made two more trips to China but this first trip with Captain Ashman seemed to open within me an inner wonder that never stopped growing."

"You had seen so much on your first voyage, Mister Dewey. I can see how you came to love the sea. It makes me imagine such adventure that I had never dreamed possible—lands I have never heard of, events that I can only read about in a book."

"Before you are too enamored with the adventure," began Samuel with a tone of caution, "I need to tell you of yet one more adventure in my first year at sea. We had gone back around the Cape of Good Hope and seemed to have an open sail back to Boston.

"It was summer, south of the equator, and we cruised on moderate breezes. Soon after we got north of the equator, however, we began to get heavy seas. We had avoided the hurricane season, which had been the captain's plan, and he had said that he expected heavier seas as we approached the Indies. What we ran into was a series of three winter storms—each more violent than that which proceeded it. It was like spasms of sea-sickness; each time we believed the worst was finally over, only to be cast again into even more violent convulsions.

"I was in charge of the aft rig, which included responsibility for the spanker. By the time that the third storm hit us, all of the forward part of the ship had been under water; the sea was pouring through the bow-ports threatening to wash everything overboard that was not attached. I had my men aloft and we double-reefed the topsails and furled all the other sails. We were aloft much of the night. At one point Captain Ashman sent the steward aloft with a glass of grog for each of the watch. I did not like grog but it was part of the life of a sailor. About an hour after midnight the gale heightened another time and we again reefed the topsails. The sea was running higher and higher. We were almost pinned to the rigging. Each time it was longer taking in the rigging, which was stiff and wet. We were cold and nearly blinded by the storm. By the time we got down on deck the brig was plunging madly into a towering head sea.

"Just then the mate who was standing atop the windless called out to furl the jib as an urgent instruction delivered to anyone on deck. Jeremiah immediately stepped forward and jumped on the bowsprit with me close behind him, not to be outdone. The rest of the crew was hauling at the jib while Jeremiah and I got out on the weather side of the jib-boom with our feet on the foot ropes and holding on by the spar. The jib was flying off to the leeward and whipping so hard we were in serious danger. For what seemed like an hour we could do nothing but hold on. The wind and sea were so furious that any call for aid or instruction was lost.

"The ship was plunged into two successive deep seas and each time we were up to our necks in water. We could hardly tell if we were still connected with the ship. Then the ship would rise up high and we would be in the air dripping water. The third time we went under I was exhausted and I knew I was losing my grip on the spar. Jeremiah could see my condition and, though again he called for help, no one could make out his words.

"Going down the water was forcing me up but I could feel one hand was loose and as the ship rose, my other hand rose. I was forced down so that my left foot became entangled in the foot ropes. I flew out and up like Old Glory on the topmost pole. Jeremiah made a one-handed pass as I came around, but I was spinning so that he missed me. I swung out and around again and he caught my passing arm and hauled me toward his body. All he could do at that second to save me and himself was to toss me to the side of the bowsprit and cross his body over mine as he grasped again the spar. In such a death-grip we rode out the fury of the next quarter hour before we could be hauled back to deck.

"Jake, I had many more similar dangerous moments at sea, but none that could pass that night off Africa. A crew of sailors who have shared such scenes and been placed in such danger, know that other crew members will automatically risk their own safety to save them. Danger is a condition at sea, not an experience. Men living in such a constant, learn to value each other as they might never do with anyone on shore. Trial and testing will come in life and neither can be overcome with fear. They should be faced in such a way that the survivor is changed for the better.

"At home I gave my mother her choice of the silks I had bought in China and then I sold the rest for a very good profit. With that and the pay I earned for the seven months at sea, I was able to give my mother $300 in silver, which was a fortune for us. I considered myself redeemed from any selfish guilt I had felt for having gone to sea. It was not the money, but the ability I had earned to provide for her. It seemed to be a secondary rite of passage."

Chapter Five

The Sea Captain and the Khedive of Egypt

Perhaps telling Jake the story of the execution was a test of the limits Samuel intended to take in his tales of adventure and discovery. Was it acceptable to tell a boy such a story without the supervision, or at least the permission of his mother? Samuel had been a boy but he had never been a parent. The event was real in his own life at a time when he had been not much older than Jake. Still he would have been very ashamed if somehow he had judged Jake's maturity incorrectly, if he had taken a liberty which had not been his right to assume. He could only wonder. Jake never gave him any indication that the story had disturbed him.

For three years Samuel had served as a midshipman under Captain Ashman. He always deemed it the most thorough training possible and he felt comfortable to assume command himself as captain of his own ship after just three years.

"Jake, I was so sure of myself at sixteen that I knew I was ready for command. You may think at that age, it would not be possible for a boy to command a sailing ship and crew on his own. Understand, however, that then it was quite common for boys who had gone to sea at twelve or thirteen, to be captains of ships by sixteen or seventeen. I knew that, but my particular confidence came from the training I had received under Captain Ashman. My friend Jeremiah already had his first ship and we had been trained together. With Captain Ashman's recommendation, I applied to the Boston shipping firm owned by William and Henry Lincoln, and, although I was accepted for future command, my first assignment was as first mate on the *Topaz*, which was a well-known whaling ship. In New England, whaling was recognized as dangerous, but the public also considered it very romantic. We sailed out of New Bedford. I recall that we had about twenty men, among whom were a number of Negroes who had run away from slavery in the South, and as free men had found a good life at sea.

"As first mate I was quartered in the forecastle with most of the crew. The quarters were close and unpleasant and it was there I began to hear for the first time about the abomination of slavery. I should have begun right then to write down some of the horrible stories I heard of beatings—feet, ears and hands chopped off, of families separated forever at the whim of the plantation owner, of brutal hours of labor in the fields. I had never been exposed to the reality of slavery and I had a difficult time imagining any system under which one person could do such things to another without fear of punishment. On some of the primitive islands to which I had already sailed, I had taken notice of people that were called slaves but I guess I considered them just a class of people in that particular society. When I heard at night such tales from the sailor in the hammock beside me, it all became personal and I was sympathetic to the suffering slave.

"Attached to the *Topaz* were small six-man boats, double-ended, called blubber-hunters, from which the whales were sought and harpooned. Besides the captain and cook, the *Topaz* carried a carpenter, harpooners and a cooper. The carpenter and cooper were responsible for assembling and fixing the oil casks. The harpooners were specially trained to be able to strike the whale with as near to a deadly blow as possible, and that took skill and great strength. Once a whale had been hit, it could drag one of these little boats for hours at a time. This wild ride was of course very hazardous. The sailors called it a 'Nantucket-sleigh-ride.' After being gaffed, the whale 'sounded,' but as it lost strength, it would come back to the surface where it could be harpooned again. In the deeper ocean, the sperm whale was known to dive to the depth of a mile. It was the sperm whale from which came the most valuable oil called 'spermacetti' which made the finest lamp oil and candles. Once dead the whale was towed to the *Topaz* and was tied to the ship with other dead whales to be taken to port for processing. When the Topaz went into the Pacific hunting whales, it was fitted with a 'tryworks' that allowed the processing of the blubber on the ship and the storage of the oil in large casks. They were not used on the two sailings that I was on in the Atlantic. Boston had a monopoly for the whale oil product in Europe at that time.

Typical Brig in full sail

"The teeth and bones of the whale were used for making products the sailors could sell: chess sets, art objects, bone handles, and 'scrimshaw.'" Samuel pointed across the room. "Look over there on the shelf, Jake. Hand me those things that look like teeth."

Jake was up and moving. "I saw them." He held one up and turned to Samuel. "They're teeth, aren't they?"

"Yes, they are—whale teeth. I rarely knew a sailor who had not learned to carve scrimshaw.

"This one was done for me by Jobo Casteen, one of those run-away slaves I told you about. I got him to carve the history of his life as he had told it to me. See, there is his master's house and then this row of little houses where the slaves lived. You see the slaves in the fields over here. Here was Jobo and his family in front of their cabin when the master told him he was going to be sold 'down South.' Here he shows himself running from the dogs. This other tooth is one I did myself. I got very good at carving on the whale teeth but I didn't try to do other objects."

"What story are you telling on this one?" Jake asked.

"This is when we harpooned our first whale. You see that the whale has been harpooned already and he is diving under the water. He has flipped the boat from which he was harpooned up in the air and the end has broken off. You see the second boat also trying to harpoon the whale. We lost one of our boy-sailors that day."

Jake was studying the scrimshaws meticulously as if checking out both the story and the technique. He did not seem, however, to be longing for a life at sea. Samuel came to the conclusion that the boy was trying instead to imagine if he could have gone away from home at such a young age to such dangerous places.

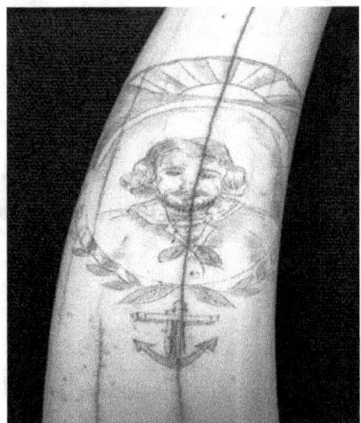

Scrimshaw art

"Two other products came from the whale," continued Samuel. "I don't have any examples, but one was called 'baleens,' made from the whale's bones and used for making the hoops that in those days held up a woman's skirt; later, something very similar was used in corsets that were called 'stays,' or 'umbrella ribs,' or even 'furniture springs.' You see, the bones were very strong but flexible.

"The last whale product was the most profitable and was called 'ambergris.' It is almost as valuable as gold. It is a substance formed inside the intestinal track of the sperm whale. When a whale swallows a giant squid it also swallows the beak of the squid which is very hard for the whale to digest. So the whale intestines secrete a substance that covers that portion of the beak to make it easier for it to go through the intestines. That very rare substance, when extracted from the dead whale, is used to set or fix perfume essences—ambergris. It is one of the ingredients that make good perfume very expensive.

"I was glad to have the experience of whaling, I presume in part, because I knew my father had once sailed on whalers and it seemed to be something we shared. What I did not enjoy was the actual experience of the harpooning and processing of the whale. Everything about that seemed to me to be dirty and unpleasant. Although the actual harpooning and processing of the carcass took some skill, I was a sailor and whaling seemed to place little value on those sailing skills.

"After about a year I was made Captain, on a temporary basis, of the *Thompson*, a square-rigged, topsail schooner. Her Captain had been injured seriously in an accident on the dock in Kingston, Jamaica. I was put in charge for most of one year during which we made regular trips back and forth to West Indies ports. These voyages were generally uneventful but unpopular with the crew because it was so common to be taken by 'yellow jack,' a fever that, just in the short time we were there, took the lives of four of our boys. Ships sailing from the West Indies were received cautiously in New England ports because they so frequently carried yellow fever that could easily erupt in an epidemic on the mainland.

"My chance to really command came when I was made captain of the *Messenger*, in eighteen twenty-four. She was a brig, like the *Guilford*, and I had my first full command just two months before my eighteenth birthday. A ship's captain, in either the navy or the merchant marine, was a respected profession in all the ports of the world. Captains made decisions on crew and cargo. In foreign ports they were sought out by brokers and tradesmen and were welcome in local society. My uniform marked me out as a man with whom to reckon in spite of my obvious youth."

Jake was enthralled. Samuel imagined he was seeing himself as the young captain in all the stories he was being told, because he could not imagine the old man as a boy. It was an easy transference. Samuel could see it in the boy's eyes. As Samuel went on with the story, he could tell Jake's mind absorbed it into the setting as he imagined it to be. Samuel would add a fact and Jake would mentally alter the setting. What Samuel said he felt, he knew Jake could also feel. Samuel's words were taken in ownership by the boy, and his expressions and body language told Samuel they were given an even bolder slant. The boy was spirited from this little room in Philadelphia onto a brig in the Atlantic with him, the windswept sea-spray lacing their faces, the deck heaving beneath their feet. Samuel enjoyed watching Jake's imaginary exploits occurring in his mind, then continued with his tale.

"It was late August when we set sail loaded with molasses, iron, and tobacco. We were on the summer Atlantic route to Gibraltar and the Mediterranean. The crew numbered eighteen, of which seven were boys around fourteen years, all of whom had already been to sea at least once. I had to resist any camaraderie with these younger crew members or lose all the respect of the older sailors. I could appear to fall into no age category. I was the Captain and I was in command. It might sound like I was acting—playing a role—and I guess there was an element of that in the relationship. I had a role to play, but it had been conferred on me by the owners of this ship. The safety, condition, pay, discipline, and reputation of this vessel lay with my success. No one sought to replace me or to assume all the responsibility that had been placed on me. The others on the ship were best served with my absolute success. I will tell you Jake, it is a fast way to grow up.

"My first mate was Levy Anderson from Salem and he was nearly twice my age. He had been a seaman since he was fifteen. He took my commands with complete confidence, never anticipating me or questioning my actions. We talked together a lot at night as brothers of the sea. There were ways he passed on advice to me in those conversations and we came to work as a command structure. There were two midshipmen: Seth Wadsworth and Simon Dickenson, both sons of sea captains who would one day become captains themselves. They were far better informed than I had been as a midshipman, and they could already pull their weight with the crew.

"The *Messenger* was called a packet boat because it was part of a fleet of ships that kept a modified schedule so that shipping schedules could be more dependable and organized. One of the things that made scheduling possible was the modification of some sailing ships to have a steam-driven paddle wheel. Under sail, one of the uncontrollable conditions was lack of wind. No headway could be made in a becalmed sea, but with the paddle wheel it was possible in such situations to still make progress. Once steam propulsion was used as a supplement, Jake, it was obvious that the days of the sailing ship as a staple of commerce were numbered. Under sail, the *Messenger* was still a brig, but more frequently she was also referred to as a packet-steamer.

"She had been built in eighteen twenty as part of the Peabody fleet. I took command four years later after she had been modified. When I first saw her, I always told people, 'I fell in love.' She had a bright lemon waist against a dark blue topside, and inside the bulwarks she was a buff color highlighted with black. I approached her first from the stern and saw the gingerbread carving painted lemon against that deep blue. I took her measure walking slowly down her starboard side to the bow which was plain-cut and handsome.

"I am sure that my great pride at the sight of this ship was the fact that I was to command; and as commander, I was to share in the profit, something I had only enjoyed in a partial way on the *Thompson*. Jake, it is called a 'vested interest,' meaning that now I was not only paid as a sailor, but I would profit in addition by the overall success of the trade that we would propagate on each voyage. If I could make better time, or negotiate a very profitable cargo at some foreign port, I would share in that profit. Everybody connected with the sea trade knew this to be the lot of the sea-captain so he was a respected man at sea and in port. Merchants sought him out. National representatives seeking trade entertained him. He was known to have money and to have authority to make decisions.

"You see this book?" Samuel said as he opened for Jake a well-worn book filled with numbers and charts. "This is my copy of Nathaniel Bowditch's *Practical Navigator*. In my time it had become the encyclopedia of navigation that all American captains used. It defined navigation and oceanography and meteorology with charts and definitions and mathematical calculations."

Samuel could see that the book meant nothing to Jake but words and numbers, and the boy could relate it to no practical purpose. "I don't expect you to be able to make use of such a book. I won't send it home with you to read. Don't worry. Can you imagine that for centuries, sailors at sea have been surrounded by water and sky, and in the sky, stars? Beginning in only primitive trials they found ways to read the sky for signs of weather changes and the stars for keys to direction. This book captures all that accumulated knowledge. That is why I call it an encyclopedia. That is what it was to me as a twenty-two-year-old sea captain.

"The voyages to Europe were not as dangerous as those that required circling one of the great south capes. The weather could be treacherous in season. As a packet ship, we now took passengers and added to my job was the care and comfort of sometimes demanding and unreasonable paying customers. There was a forty-five foot main cabin for general use with eight staterooms about ten feet square. There was a wine and spirit room, a very small library and a bathing room. Passengers had their own covered deck behind the mainmast all served by four stewards devoted just to the passengers. For the older sailors, such accommodations seemed unnatural to the traditions of the sea. All the raucous, hardy adventure seemed to have been discarded. Out of Boston, the *Messenger* was one of the few packet-boats that established the Liverpool route. Other companies in Boston, however, resisted the coming of steam and therefore New York, with faster and more reliable sailings, was allowed to grow in importance as a port.

"Liverpool was as important as London as a commercial center for England. My first impression of it was that of an international city because I observed right away there were many blacks in the population. I was later told that quite a few African kings sent their sons there for their education and of those, a large number stayed to build businesses. There were observable numbers of Chinese working on the docks. The city was driven by commerce, and all England was caught up in the consequences of the industrial revolution. The world was demanding English manufactured goods, and ships like ours were bringing in raw materials. I remember on one of the first trips we carried logwood from Honduras — much in demand for wine barrels, to give rich colors to Mediterranean wines. New England rum was now in demand in England and the Mediterranean. The mills of New England were producing good quality cottons that were popular throughout Europe.

"This kind of trade between Boston and Liverpool took on an air of monotony, repetition, and routine that was typical of the nature of manufacturing in the industrial revolution. The tradition of the sea had been a struggle between man and the mastery of the elements through which the better, the craftier, the more experienced was likely to prevail. The eighteenth century manufacturer was a craftsman who used his acquired skill to convert raw materials into useful products that could not readily be made on the farm. I did not appreciate these changing trends. I sought skill and enjoyed adventure and struggle.

"To my great pleasure, the *Messenger's* assignment was shifted from the Liverpool packet trade to the Mediterranean where it was hoped a similar packet trade could be developed. New York ships were already sailing on modified schedules to Mediterranean ports. We called at Gibraltar, Malaga, Marseilles, Genoa, Leghorn, Gallipoli, Messina, Palermo, Trieste, Volvo, Salonika, Malta, Jaffa, and Alexandria. Marseilles was to be our packet-port, the destination into which we would put on each voyage on some kind of schedule. We had latitude on our schedule so that if we were short on return consignments, we could call at other ports to supplement our cargo. In this way we were also able to test the trade of these various ports and their potential as stronger markets in the future. This gave me added responsibility as captain, since the company was trusting me to be able to evaluate markets, to make business contacts, to negotiate with men of diverse nationalities. In spite of my youth, I never felt that I was not respected. As an American, I had already found that I was regarded as more aggressive, less ready to act stubbornly on tradition. In most of the foreign ports this was strange, but it was tolerated because the trade of the Americans was always aggressively sought.

"In the Mediterranean there was still adventure to be experienced. In Salonika, which is a Greek city, I was once captured by thieves in an open street. In spite of my cries, I was abducted into an alley doorway and to a cellar where I was bound. Since I had just come from negotiations with a Greek broker, I immediately believed that he was somehow involved in this abduction. I was quickly robbed of the gold in my pockets, but it was obvious the thieves believed there was more to be had for my person. My crew reported me missing when I didn't return on schedule, but no authority was willing yet to take any action. That night I was removed, under close guard, to a small boat in the harbor.

"There was very little communication because I knew no Greek and my captors knew no English but it became obvious overnight, in the course of some coming and going, that the thieves had encountered problems. What I did not know then was that these incompetents had mistaken me for an English ship-captain who, it appeared, was engaged in some nefarious dealings of his own and had been sought by rivals. The thieves found that the rival group wanted nothing to do with an American sailor and would offer nothing for me as a captive. Now the thieves had no market for their product and their choice was to kill me or to let me go. I was not aware they were considering those particular alternatives, but I did see that they were no longer watching me so closely. Scanning the room, I saw nearby a metal rod in the floor and was able to get close enough to work the rod into the ropes that bound my hands. With as little obvious motion as possible, I loosened the rope enough to slide my hands free. I waited until I felt the thieves were as diverted as possible by other concerns, then I sprang up and through the lone gangway door.

"Once on deck I had little time to search the dark horizon for my next destination, but seeing only lights of another much larger ship, I dove into the suddenly icy cold black water. I could hear the consternation on the little boat from which I had fled, but was relieved that no one sought to pursue me further. I swam more regularly toward this bigger ship which I thought was rather garishly lit. The port gangway was pulled up to a neutral levee, but with several attempts I was able to thrust myself out of the water enough to grab the bottom rung and pull myself up. There I rested and considered my position.

"I had gotten free of my captors, whoever they were. I was now on the ladder of another ship of unknown nationality, having lost all my identity except my soaking uniform. I decided not to call out but to climb the ladder and announce myself to the unknown crew. I dripped a while longer, but was getting no warmer, so I climbed the ladder and stepped onto the deck. I was spotted almost immediately by a crewman who called out an alarm in a language I did not know. In an instant I was surrounded by five sailors, each armed.

"I told them in English that I was Captain Samuel Wentworth Dewey, commander of the American ship *Messenger*. I believe I could have told them that I was the King of Siam and I would have gotten the same hostile, bland expressions. More sailors crowded around and finally a man whom I took to be an officer. Their uniforms were blue with red trim, their pants were pantaloons, and they wore a red fez, a conical hat with a blue tassel. I announced myself again to the officer and was directed by hand motions to follow, which I did, surrounded by this gaggle of suspicious sailors.

"Below deck I was taken to a most commodious stateroom and entered with this crowd around me all bowing up and down out of sequence. I observed rather critically that the bowing was submissive as opposed to a formal diplomatic bow and I did not participate. Before me lounged about a dozen potentates in garish costumes on chairs that looked more like small beds. The commander of my captors stepped forward and prostrated himself before one of the viziers, was recognized, and made a formal statement, obviously about me.

"At this point the bearded man, beside what appeared to be the head-man, spoke to me in distinct, academic English. He asked me who I was, and again I introduced myself as I had twice before. Then he asked why I had come aboard the 'Khedive's ship' without invitation. I explained my abduction and escape and that I did not know whose ship I had presumed upon, but I considered it the duty of any honorable ship to rescue a fellow sailor in such distress. The man communicated all this to the group, who began to speak among themselves in what I thought was a relaxed manner. That was reassuring to me. Then I was told that I had come aboard the *Akidar*, the private yacht of the Khedive of Egypt, Mohammed Ali. I was an intruder, but as a naval officer in distress, I would be held for the American *Chargé d'Affaire* in Salonika.

Mohammed Ali, Khedive of Egypt

"Then, as if all that was a formality, the Khedive motioned me forward and he welcomed me in the same precise English as had his secretary. He said I was his welcome guest and I should go with a servant girl so that I could get some dry clothes. I would be his guest at dinner. This girl took me to an exquisite guest room where three women, whose faces were covered by their robes, and a man, gave me a brilliant robe, my own fez and shoes, and took my wet clothes to be cleaned. Had I been transformed for a play? Was I a prince or mere entertainment? When I returned to the Khedive's stateroom, a bench had been placed for me between the Khedive and the secretary, Ali Marmon.

"Our feast was magnificent and we had fine wines and cakes. Afterwards we were entertained by exotic dancers and smoked from a *nargile,* a kind of water pipe that stood about four feet high. My conversation was only with the Khedive and Ali Marmon. I believe they alone could speak English. I learned that the Khedive had ruled since eighteen oh five as part of the Ottoman Empire. The Ottomans had ended the last Egyptian Caliphate in the sixteenth century soon after the fall of Constantinople.

"The Khedive had a keen interest in America. He questioned me in detail about our people and our government form. He had read our constitution several times but had found it alien to any government with which he was familiar. His speculation was that we were a different type of people in America. Although we had slaves, we let people from across the water come into our country as one of us—without invasion. 'How can that be?' he said. We spoke about Jesus and Mohammed and then about Abraham. I recognized that academically he was much my superior so I was careful not to let myself assume the role of an authority on any of our subjects. It was a pleasant surprise to me that a kind of bond in depth grew between us. We were completely free of any measure of master and slave, accepting each other as men of our own element. He was occasionally paternal, but not attempting any superiority, only appreciating my youth and perhaps my enthusiasm.

"I did not know until the next day that, while we talked so congenially, the Khedive's men were investigating my story through whatever were their sources. For the second time in less than two days men had debated my fate without my knowledge. Had I not turned out to be whom I purported to be, I surely would have been executed or at the very least imprisoned indefinitely for my presumption. As it happened, the next day I was returned in the Khedive's launch to the *Messenger*, much to the surprise and satisfaction of my crew."

"Were you scared, Mr. Dewey?" Jake's expression was incredulous, as though everything he had just heard was beyond his comprehension.

"Funny thing about 'scared,' Jake. You have to know or sense danger before you get scared. I never knew anyone was debating my harm. You've heard the saying, 'What you don't know can't hurt you,' haven't you?"

"Yes sir."

"Well, I am living proof of that. But by the same manner it could be added that a fool and his head are soon parted. I was too ignorant to know the danger I was in."

Samuel tossed an open palm in the air. "Anyway, out of all this came a cherished friendship. I was invited to Alexandria and went there on my next voyage at the urging of my company. They had provided me all kinds of gifts for the Khedive and I was able to negotiate the first trade agreements with his government and an American company. After that, Alexandria became my packet destination in the Mediterranean, and through Khedive Mohammed Ali I established special trade arrangements in Jaffa, Malta, Smyrna, and Constantinople.

"I was not alone in the development of this rich trade in the eastern Mediterranean. A favorite port was Smyrna, where Boston ships connected with trade from the Orient. Streets in Smyrna teemed with Kurd, Anatolian, Armenian, Frank, and Greek, all under the benevolent rule of the Ottomans. Sun-dried fruits, course wool for the New England mills, as well as gum-arabic and tragacanth, both essential to cotton printing, were in abundance. Turkish carpets, sponges, drugs such as myrrh and scammony, sought by American doctors, and almonds and cypress wood all were sought to fill the holds of our ships by then empty of our Yankee products. As I toured the merchant stalls I was introduced each time to new, more exotic products, and with each I tried to learn all I could about its source and applications. Jake, you might imagine it as Mister Ridley Hamilton's candy shop where I am sure you have gone to look over his product."

Jake nodded his head with a knowing smile.

"The choices seem limitless, and since all choices are good, the wise choice is not the one you know, but the new one that surprises you with new flavor. I must admit that sometimes my company found fault with my tendency for the exotic, but I dare say I introduced a number of new tastes and products to Boston society as a ship captain.

"Jake, I cannot tell you of all the sights that were opened to me at this time. See that statue of the man over there—the white marble, there, there," Samuel said as he pointed. "This is a Greek carving from the time of Christ. I was awarded this in Constantinople as a special gift because they thought it was a Christian relic, and as an American, I was automatically in their eyes a Christian. I am sure that it is valuable, but I prize it as a symbol of the many religions of the East.

"In Constantinople, I must tell you of the great Mosque of Santa Sophia—Divine Wisdom. Constantinople is the capital of the Ottoman Empire whose armies captured the city in fourteen fifty-three in one of the great climactic events of western history. Originally it was built by the Roman Emperor Constantine as his capital in the East of the Mediterranean—with Rome as his capital in the West. After Rome fell to invasion, the Emperors continued to rule in the East, and the Emperor Justinian built this great cathedral. Constantinople became the greatest city in the world. It was ruled by Greek Christians and was a revered religious and commercial city which attracted riches and glory. The church was considered to rival Saint Peter's in Rome and to have exceeded the Temple of Solomon in Jerusalem. It is said that on the day Constantinople fell to the Moslem army of Mohammed the Second, as many as one hundred thousand Greek Christians crowded into Santa Sophia, believing desperately that God would not let his church fall to the invaders. It was not to be.

"The doors were broken open and the people slaughtered. Altars and crucifixes, mosaics and statues were smashed and Mohammed the Second stood on the altar and declared, 'There is no God but Allah, and Mohammed is his prophet.' After that bloody day, the great church was converted to a mosque and minarets defined its purpose.

"It is difficult for any person to capture in any language the experience of entering Santa Sophia. The entrance is onto a vast, stretching threshold of many colors of carpet laid one upon the other, and noiselessly you pass into a domed space that extends up one hundred eighty-two feet. The central dome, more than one hundred feet in diameter, appears suspended weightless upon a circle of forty windows. The dome is carried on four concave triangular sections of masonry supported by four huge piers at the corners to take the weight of the dome. The incredible result is the impression of suspension. There are no side aisles or buttresses, characteristic of support as in early European cathedrals.

Saint Sophia in Constantinople

"The tale is told that in the tenth century, when Santa Sophia was still a Christian place of worship, the Grand Prince of Russia sought to choose which of the three great faiths: Islam, Christianity, or Judaism, that he should force upon his people, he sent emissaries to Mecca, Constantinople, and Jerusalem to see what each faith had to offer. The delegates sent to Constantinople, on entering Santa Sophia, were so overwhelmed by this magnificent church that they declared this surely must be heaven, and the Russian people were baptized into Eastern Christianity.

"Now, the interior has undergone change again, and is covered in colorful marbles with golden mosaics and Arabic letters with the names of Allah and Mohammed. All the Christian decorations that the Russian delegates once saw as heavenly are destroyed or covered over. Today it is again a Moslem shrine, an operating mosque where visitors are welcome."

Jake's face again looked as if it had been left ajar, as if he had stopped trying to control his body, so captured was his imagination. Samuel was certain that Jake could not truly envision the sights he'd described without seeing it himself or seeing pictures, but the boy's unbridled attention and fascination showed he was measuring every word that he might connect with the concepts that Samuel projected. Samuel chuckled to himself. Of course it was impossible, but the sheer exercise had seemed to inflate the size of Jake's head.

Then, as if to give Jake no relief for his pulsing curiosity, Samuel continued. "Of all the wonders of the East to which I was exposed by my friendship with the Khedive, none was more bizarre or befuddling to me than my visit to another place of Christian pilgrimage in the city of Jerusalem. That was the place where was buried the body of the crucified Jesus—the Church of the Holy Sepulcher."

"You saw where they buried Jesus, Mister Dewey? Really?"

"Well yes, Jake, and where Abraham was buried, and Solomon's Temple, and the place where Jesus was crucified, and the Garden of Gethsemane, and all the places I had heard about as a child when my mother read to me from the Bible. Whatever I had imagined then was a completely different reality when it was pointed out to me in the Holy Land.

"But, Jake, you must understand that it is two thousand years since those events. Much of what is today shown to tourists is only known by tradition and cannot be proven as accurate. It is human nature that much 'proof' simply comes from tradition. Hand me that box over there on the shelf, wrapped by the two gold bands."

Jake complied but as he did he wondered aloud, half to himself, "I never knew if those places were real places or not. I guessed that they were part of the story but I could never see them as real."

Samuel opened the lidded box with a perceptible reverence. He lifted out first what Jake saw immediately was a cross.

"This wooden cross, I was told," he said to Jake as if disclosing a secret, "was carved from a piece of the cross on which Jesus was crucified." He handed it toward Jake but the boy made no move to take it.

"Go ahead. To me it is a treasure among many other treasures. Think about it, Jake. There was a table with many of these carved crucifixes, and if for two thousand years they had been carving them from pieces of the cross, how big would the cross of Jesus have had to have been? In this little box here," he said as he lifted another small box from inside the bigger treasure box, "is a piece of cloth sold to me as part of the robe of Mary. Here is a small stone that I picked up beside the Wailing Wall that was once part of Solomon's Temple. I could tell you it was part of that wall, but all I really know is that it is a rock and where I found it.

"The things in this box are treasures of my several visits to the Holy Land. They are memories for me, nothing more. They also remind me of why I remember my visit to the Church of the Holy Sepulcher as so befuddling.

"The building is an unimpressive stone structure built by Constantine about three hundred years after the crucifixion. Within the walls of this church seem to be located all the sites connected with the life of Jesus that could have been located in Jerusalem. The various divisions of Christianity are in charge of one or more of these places. Because these groups are so hostile to each other it is necessary for the Turkish government to maintain guards there to keep them from killing each other. These little chapels mark the place where Jesus' body was anointed, the place where Mary stood while His body was anointed, the place where Jesus' garments were distributed by lot, where Jesus received the crown of thorns, where He was scourged, where He was nailed to the cross, where He appeared to Mary Magdalene, and where the centurions stood. Not far away is the Chapel of the Crucifixion and the tomb of Adam.

The most revered place in the building is the Holy Sepulcher. It is a small chapel built of highly polished limestone measuring twenty-six by eighteen feet. The chapel is a room within a room. Pilgrims, and in this case I was a pilgrim, advanced toward the entrance in a disorganized line. Some people were weeping and moaning, waiting their turn. When it was my turn to go in, I entered a small vestibule hung with gilded lamps. Encased before me was a piece of rock which was identified as the rock rolled away from the tomb of Jesus. I went further into a marble-lined compartment about seven feet by six feet. The air was repressive because the ceiling was hung with forty-three golden lamps kept constantly burning. Of these lamps, thirteen belong to the Catholics, thirteen to the Greek Orthodox, thirteen to the Armenians and four to the Coptic Church.

Church of the Holy Sepulchre - Jerusalem

"Then I passed into an inner room which was supposed to be the actual tomb of Christ. In the middle was a marble slab on which His body was laid and it was worn perfectly smooth by the centuries of pilgrims who have reverently kissed it. When I came out of the chapel I looked around at the collection of pilgrims who awaited entrance and I was reminded of a saying told me the day before I visited the tomb: 'If thy neighbor has made one pilgrimage, distrust him; if he has made two, make haste to sell your house.'

"It was this same skeptic who described to me what happens every Easter at this little church: the miracle of the 'Holy Fire.' This tradition has been discarded by all but the Orthodox. During the entire day and night before Easter, the church is packed with people standing for hours without food or drink. They work themselves into a frenzy chanting 'This is the tomb of the Lord.' As the sacred moment approaches people press toward the little chapel and even climb on the backs of other pilgrims. At two o'clock in the afternoon the Greek Patriarch goes into the tomb. There is a strange silence and then the whispered word that the Holy Ghost has descended on the Sepulcher and a half dozen lighted torches are thrust through holes in the chapel walls. Like maniacs, thousands of people struggle to get their tapers lit from the flames. As many as three hundred pilgrims have been known to be trampled at one single such celebration.

"Jake, I can do nothing except describe for you what I saw and was told. I am neither priest nor preacher. I cannot explain further. I can say that it was an unforgettable experience that I will never fully understand. I cannot profess it as the hand of God but as the hysteria of believers about whom I have little right to make judgment."

Chapter Six

South America

For the next few days Jake would not be diverted from his questions about Samuel's experiences as a sea captain. It was not that he had so many treasures to show Jake of his time at sea, but that the boy's imagination seemed to be tethered to the subject, unwilling to set Samuel free. Samuel mused later, remembering this time with Jake, "I was willing to let him dictate this pace, for his comfort, but it also was a pleasure for me to relive my experiences with someone who sincerely wanted to hear about them." There was no glazing of Jake's eyes as a tale grew long. Instead, if there were danger or excitement, his eyes might enlarge and his face become animated. Samuel seemed at these times to be something of a puppeteer.

It also came to him that his plan to let Jake find a treasure that piqued his interest and then give him the story from Samuel's life, was not working as well as the older man might have liked. It seemed more natural in the process just to tell of those experiences in sequence and allow him to search or observe the treasures that went with that part of the story. Samuel decided that it was more important for Jake to be able to place such tales in time, in Samuel's life sequence, because then his imagination could conjure that experience in relation to the setting. The objects, instead of initiating the story, were more useful to Jake to illustrate or illuminate what his mind was already processing. When he held an object at that point it was as if he were saying to himself, "So this is it or so this came from that place."

Finally, Samuel picked up the story again. "By the time I was about twenty-five, I was beginning to tire of my life at sea. I have told you how that life was changing. I still was enthusiastic about the relationship I had with the Khedive of Egypt and the many amazing connections that I had through him all over the Islamic world. In the shipping company, this friendship was considered a valuable asset and I was always given more flexibility in negotiating for cargo than the other captains. Tales got out about my friendship, and my reputation in Boston grew. Somehow, however, my company became aware of my declining interest in the sea, and as an alternative to the Mediterranean voyages, I was offered another ship which was assigned to the South America trade. I was intrigued because liberation movements throughout that continent had created new governments, all seeking to build trade in their own interests instead of as part of the Spanish or Portuguese Empires that had ruled them for hundreds of years.

"On my final sailing to the Mediterranean, I had arranged to stay several days in Alexandria, and the Khedive insisted that I be his guest. I was not, by tradition, allowed to enter into his harem but he provided me with a harem of my own to service my every need. At one point when we were in a discussion of the differences in the way our respective societies approached life, he asked me if I would like to select one of the beautiful women from the harem he had provided to me, as a wife and as a gift from him. Jake, that's one of the treasures that I did not bring home. I told Mohammed Ali that his offer was indeed generous and the women were all beautiful, but I was returning to my society where such arrangements were not allowed. If I took a woman into that situation, it would be a very unhappy experience for her. He asked me, 'but would it be a happy experience for you?' When I told him that it would, he was not able to comprehend why the happiness of the woman would even be considered."

Jake interrupted. "Mister Dewey, if you did not accept the gift of a wife, did you ever marry? I have not heard you mention either a wife or children."

Samuel paused before answering his question. "No, Jake, I have never had either wife or children. I might place that at the top of the list of what I would call the disappointments of my life. I am not sorry that I did not take the Khedive's offer, but as I look back, I believe that I would have liked to have had a wife, and children might be a great pleasure to me now. I have had a number of close female friendships and more than one romance, but somehow each time my nature has seemed to take me away from the prospect of domestic tranquility through the lure of new adventure or a new investment. In a long life such as I have had, it is certainly possible to have a family and adventure. For some men that is double adventure. But my life never evolved in that fashion."

He avoided telling the boy that the early death of his father and the difficulty that his mother went through in raising four children, made him overly cautious whenever he considered marriage. His going to sea at twelve and beginning his adventurous life was precisely the result of the problems his mother was having in taking care of him. Jake's father too had died early, been killed, and had left his mother with the total responsibility for the care and upbringing of her children. Had Samuel said more, Jake's very agile mind would sense the obvious similarity of their experiences, and in spite of himself, Samuel might have then provided an unintended influence. He therefore added no further comment at that time.

"At the end of my visit the Khedive presented me with a very special gift." He walked over to the covered closet and rummaged in the back. The box that he brought out was blue leather decorated in gold with Islamic lettering. He sat down and Jake drew very near with expectation as he opened the lid of the box.

"This gold sword was from the Khedive's treasury. The jewels are real and the workmanship is flawless. He told me that it had come from the Seljug Persian Empire in the Twelfth Century at the time of the First Christian Crusades. I saw that although the chest was decorated with Islamic script, the gold sword had no such markings. Then he said very formally, 'I am returning it to a very peaceful Christian Crusader and friend.'"

He handed the sword over to Jake who took it with appropriate reverence. Samuel doubted that Jake heard anything else the old man said for several minutes. "The New England harpoon and three cases of spermacetti whale oil that I had brought as a gift seemed mundane in comparison with the Khedive's gift."

Jake stared at the sword then said, "May I take it out, Mister Dewey, if I'm real careful?"

"Of course you can."

Jake took out the sword with delicate care but in another minute he was twirling it around in an imaginary sword fight with pirates. Samuel left him alone for a few moments in his reverie. "Our secret now, Jake, not to tell anyone. Remember."

"Oh, I won't tell no one, Mister Dewey. I promise!" the boy said as he parried and thrust.

The next day, Samuel told Jake about his new ship, the *Israel*. "She was a full rigged ship just four years old and was the largest ship our company had yet sent to be part of the South America trade. Unlike the brigs that I had sailed, the *Israel* had a third or mizzenmast from which the spanker was set. As I said, I was intrigued with the prospect of sailing in new waters and seeing other lands and the command of another, larger ship had some appeal.

"Independence had brought a new age to the countries of South America. Fledgling democracies were notoriously unstable and the colonial powers had not left those states with strong, educated middle classes on which to build political or economic independence. In most countries patrician families, who had been a support to colonial rulers, now had quickly and opportunistically filled the vacuum that followed independence and controlled their regions themselves. I think that it appealed to my company that I had been so successful in the Mediterranean in creating strong bonds with those who controlled the local commerce. No doubt they looked for me to accomplish the same adaptation in the countries of South America and I had already considered that prospect. So, as the *Israel* set sail, my intentions were all bound up in a new ship and new markets in trade.

"Out of Boston the *Israel* sailed down the coast and around the Carolina cape, turned southeast to the Cape Verde Islands, very near the route I had taken on voyages to the Far East. At the islands, we picked up the northeast trade winds that could clear us of the northeast promontory of Brazil, to the Equator where we found the more southerly trade winds. Although later trips would take us to Guiana, Venezuela, and New Granada, our destination on our first voyage was Brazil, which was now an Empire ruled by the son of the King of Portugal.

"It interested me that when Revolution came to South America, it was the Portuguese king who accepted it and peacefully led the people into their own empire. What might indeed have happened if King George had suggested that alternative to the men of Boston in seventeen seventy-five?

"This was the only monarchy on a continent filled with emerging republics, many still in uncertain revolution. It was difficult even for the locals to keep up with the current political situation, so we always attempted to avoid politics in our dealings, even if we came from the country that had inspired the various struggles for independence. Our rivalry was again with the British for the best trading positions that we could arrange in any one port. The British trade out of Liverpool was based on coal, which Britain had in abundance, and strangely South America had little coal.

"As we crossed the Equator, the light at night was so bright that we could almost read. I saw flying fish for the first time. They were a foot long with wings, and schools might rise out of the sea, wheel around and drop back the other way. They flew across our bow and I was told the reason for such antics was the dolphins that pursued them. Some even fell on board ship to be picked up by the crew for dinner. Near the equator we saw Portuguese Men-of-War, strange blue bubbles with long legs for oars. They rise and swell out above the water to six or seven inches in length and about the same height. Actually they resemble little ships under full sail and they would try to out-sail the *Israel*. But such bravery was soon surrendered when a wind came up and they dove under water.

"We were laden with sheeting from the power looms at Waltham, Massachusetts and pine boards from Maine, and miscellaneous trade goods even from China. It is difficult for me now to remember with accuracy the cargo of each voyage but I know that we never sailed without New England cloth. I remember lumber on this sailing because it was so strange to me when we unloaded Maine Pine and took on Honduran logwood and mahogany.

"History tells us that the Spanish/ Portuguese conquest of South America concentrated on the wealth in gold and silver there, more a robbery of wealth than an effort to establish an economy. Now the new states found other wealth in hides, coffee, iron ore, tin, oil, timber and guano—bird droppings.

"Approaching Rio de Janeiro, we saw that the clouds covered the peaks of the mountains except for Sugar Loaf, which loomed over the city, a great baguette standing on end. Brazil was still importing slaves out of Africa for their labor-intensive coffee and sugar plantations and their timber forests. Other republics had a very small proportion of slaves. In Brazil such importation was a rich trade, engaged in earlier by the British. It was a moral struggle for me to observe this tragic trade in humans, captured in Africa and brought in chains to South America and to the West Indies Islands.

"Rio was a busy port, but more than that it was a beautiful setting for a city. From there we sailed for the river Plata, first to Montevideo and then to Buenos Aires. Approaching La Plata at night we heard the strange barking up river of the sea dogs, sometimes called sea lions.

"In Rio and Montevideo I invested funds in hides and coffee which promised a good return on my speculation when we arrived back in Boston. At Buenos Aires we observed a strange phenomenon on La Plata when the wind blew all the water out of the river and it was possible for people to walk to town. It was dangerous because the wind could suddenly shift and the water would come rushing back and strand or drown anyone caught in the river bed.

"In Rio I also saw what they call the Passing of the Peace: a religious ceremony that was strange to me. In eighteen twenty, the Inquisition decreed that only the Catholic Church be recognized by the state. I observed a small boy with a 'ding dong' bell who proceeded through the street followed by pairs of soldiers with muskets and fixed bayonets, then a priest carrying a wafer and gold cup. All, everybody, had to kneel, even foreigners, and men mounted or in carriages had to dismount and kneel. As I said, it was a strange procession in contrast to my New England background and demonstrated the power of the Catholic Church in South America."

"Mister Dewey," said Jake. "You were able to see so many strange things on all your voyages. I am surprised the mystery did not keep you a sailor."

Jake was again caught up in the excitement of adventure which Samuel had encouraged with his tales. That was natural but it was not Samuel's purpose.

"By hearing about or reading about another person's life, Jake, we have to recognize that times change and we change and you cannot re-create my experiences. I tell them to you to excite your imagination, to amuse you, and to suggest that you too can make for yourself a rewarding life without imitating mine.

"I think I told you, it was in this travel to South America on the *Israel* that I took a greater interest in minerals and geology. Look here," he said, rising and going behind the half-open curtained doorway only to struggle with another wooden box on which Jake saw "South America."

"Some of these are quite dusty but very nice specimens of minerals that I found or bought over the time I was making trips to South America. Each one has a number and letters indicating where it was found." With that introduction Samuel picked up the first sample. "Here is an amethyst with calcite from Uruguay. I think that purple and green are my favorite colors in minerals."

Jake was given the stone made up of hundreds of fractures creating surfaces of varying shades of purple. He turned the stone around in his hands. It was covered in pointed corners. "Are these all made up of many gem stones?"

"They could be if someone chose to make jewelry. Remember, Jake, this is quartz, like we talked about from Stokes County, and we found some amethyst there. He picked up another. "Now this is from Peru. It is rodochrosite with quartz. It is pink, almost like a pudding, and has larger facets like little blocks all together."

Jake sat down the amethyst and picked up the pink rock turning it around in his open hand. Samuel gave him time to examine each specimen closely. They spent the afternoon and most of the next day with the box. Samuel knew that the names and details would not be retained by the boy but at one point he brought out the book in which he had recorded each numbered item and written down all the descriptive information. Jake kept the book open and each time he looked at another rock he looked it up judiciously in the book—matching the number key on the specimen with the description.

Eventually their feet were surrounded with brilliant stones in a myriad of colors: flourite, prousite, emeralds, chrysoberl, uranocircite, brazilianite, herderite, hematite, tourmaline, ribbons of silver and gold. Jake's eyes widened in amazement at this display. Finally he ventured, "Is the world covered with such riches as these, Mister Dewey?"

"My first answer, Jake, is yes. Let me qualify that by adding that a collection such as this has to be assembled from many places over a long period of time. Only in a museum might you find a range of minerals gathered together in such a way as this. In fact, this collection represents only a small fraction of the mineral wealth of this world. It is God who has poured out this abundance at our very feet. This is just one example of what the Bible says God intended when He finished with creation and declared, 'It was very good.' But it is humans who have placed another definition on wealth, meaning value. In God's world, gold and silver were good. They could be made into beautiful objects or decorations. In the world as man began to fashion it, gold and silver were prized and coveted to represent intrinsic value as worth. As a result, whole civilizations were destroyed and thousands warred with each other to possess the wealth for themselves.

"Jake, when I began to collect these specimens, it was out of wonder at their beauty, then at the amazing variety that they represented. Gradually I began to see these minerals in the same terms as the coal of England, the mahogany of Honduras, the cloth of New England—they were commodities in a world marketplace. It was in South America that I first came to wonder at their beauty, and then to see that they could be a partial means to build the weak, new economies of that continent. And you will see how, out of that, I began to invest my time in land in America and South America that was based on the mineral resources of the earth and the possibilities of trade."

Chapter Seven

Andy Jackson's Head

Samuel allowed Jake to examine the South American mineral specimens as he pondered the way he would describe for the boy the next exploit of his life—his most daring and probably least admirable. He recognized that a boy of Jake's age would imagine his actions only as swashbuckling and heroic. While he was not ashamed of what he had done, he had to admit that he had never been entirely successful in preventing his actions in 1834 from defining his entire life. *Just tell it. The boy likes a good story and he'll not condemn you.* They put away the mineral specimens and Samuel began a new story as he took a small walnut box off one of the shelves.

"Jake, in my twenty-seventh year I finally broke my association with the sea. I could just say that I resigned as Captain of the *Israel*, or that I left the Boston shipping company. I did that, but I certainly did more than that, and I need to tell you the whole story. You know the famous Navy ship, 'Old Ironsides,' that is still berthed in Boston harbor, don't you?"

"Yes, indeed I do. In school I learned to recite the poem by Mister Oliver Wendell Holmes:

'Oh, better that her shattered hulk
Should sink beneath the waves;
Her thunders shook the mighty deep,
And there should be her grave;
Nail to the mast her holy flag,
Set every threadbare sail,
And give her to the God of storms,
The lightning and the gale.'

We had pictures and all, but I never really saw 'Old Ironsides.' I bet you did, Mister Dewey."

Samuel chuckled. "Oh, I saw her all right. Of course you know that her real name was *Constitution,* and she was a frigate built in seventeen ninety-four when Congress realized the United States needed a fleet worthy of rivaling the British Navy if we were to compete in world trade. That was before I was born.

"The *USS Constitution* saw service in the war we almost had with France, and the Barbary War, and the War of Eighteen twelve, and she had a glorious record. Now when she was built, she was given a figurehead that represented Hercules standing on a firm rock. You know that a figurehead is a carved wooden statue of a person or thing that was attached to the bow of many sailing ships as decoration—to make it warlike.

"In eighteen oh four, in the harbor at Tripoli, a gust of wind blew the *Constitution* into her sister ship, *President,* and her figurehead was splintered. When the damage was repaired she got a new figurehead which was just expanding spirals connecting to the tailboard.

"In eighteen thirty-three, the *Constitution* was scheduled to be refitted in the Boston Naval Yard and it was there found that she was so badly rotted that she really needed a complete restoration. Jake, that's when Mister Holmes wrote his poem. There was a rumor that 'Old Ironsides' was about to be scrapped because restoration would be so expensive, and his poem was a protest to the Navy plan to scrap her.

USS Constitution under repair

"Along came the Commandant of the Boston Yard, Captain Jesse Duncan Elliott, whose personal hero was the President, Andrew Jackson. Elliott arranged, with a local woodcutter whom I knew, Laban Beecher, to carve a new figurehead in the form of a full length statue of President Andrew Jackson. You may not know this, but politics was a serious business in those Jackson days, and I was among those fully opposed to his policies. I told you that politics was one of my interests and I was about to get right into the middle of the most partisan kind.

"The *Israel* was in port and I was celebrating my twenty-eighth birthday with some of my friends, when we were presented with a handbill calling on citizens of Boston to prevent the desecration of what was noted as 'their' frigate, with the likeness of the hated Andrew Jackson. The president, particularly because of some of his monetary policies, was not very popular in Boston. I admit that I had drunk too much rum and I was boisterous in my outrage against this 'desecration of Old Ironsides with the graven image of Old Hickory.' I remember at one point standing upon a table with the crowd cheering my blasphemies.

Harper's Weekly - 1875

"When the rowdiness subsided and we were once again in our seats, Gamaliel Pratt, another Boston sea captain whom I had known since school, began to make light of my protests. He had known me well enough to consider me a keen practical joker. Baiting me might be a lot of fun.

"'Would a Yankee sea captain dare to take on the mighty Jackson?' he said in a louder voice than necessary, to merely get my attention. 'What have you in mind?'

"The surroundings were close and conspiratorial, not far from the image of 'a den of thieves.' Every conversation seemed to be on the very edge of dishonorable.

"Our other friends had enough gumption to bring down our volume and our rhetoric but we continued our banter. Jake, alcohol may enliven conversation and revelry, but it is a poor concoction to mix with good judgment. The latter always suffers.

"Gamaliel pressed on with a general challenge to me that should have been ignored. Instead, with a voice of intrigue, I suggested that, 'Andy Jackson would never sail on the bow of the *USS Constitution.'*"

"'I will wager,' countered Gamaliel, 'one quarter of my proceeds from my next sailing that you will find a sober mind, and as he has with so many, Old Hickory will indeed sail forth in more conquests.'

"'Done!' I cried dramatically. 'You shall have your wager, sir.' The challenge was made, but fortunately, befuddled as I was, I kept my own council. I had no idea what I would do nor of course how I would do it but I was not going to say anything further to Mister Pratt either, to encumber my alternatives or to let slip details of any plan.

"The *Israel* sailed again for Rio, and during that voyage I wrestled with my obligation. I think I was fully prepared to leave the sea, to cut that responsibility for ship and crew. Much as I disliked President Jackson, I wished him no harm. The more I pondered, the more that a certain impulsiveness seemed to overpower judgment, and once I had surrendered to the very idea of a strategy, I was committed. I deliberated the details of my plan during the rest of that voyage and returned to Boston with a fully refined enterprise. No longer did I have just a wager to be won, but I had a scenario by which I would announce to the world that I was not to be taken as just a swaggering sea captain, but a man with whom the world must now reckon.

"I found Boston as filled with protest as had been the case earlier when rumor had spread that the *Constitution* was to be destroyed. This time, the contemptuous Commodore Elliot had brought the *Constitution* from the dry dock and anchored it not twenty-five feet from the bridge at Charlestown.

"It was well known by everyone in Boston that the universal position for a ship at anchor in Charlestown harbor was pointing northeast, on account of the northeast winds. The Commodore had placed the *Constitution* with the nose of the ship pointing northwest, and between the warships *Independence* and *Columbus*—both properly facing northeast. The people of Middlesex County took this as a personal insult to their political persuasion. There was Andrew Jackson, in full likeness, 'caped' and with hat in one hand along with a copy of the US Constitution held firmly in the other, sharply visible to all. We approached the Fourth of July and I took particular note of the symbolism of that date.

"The night of July second was foul, with a heavy squall punctuated with thunder and lightning. It was a bit more weather than I had anticipated but I needed the darkness. In my cabin I dressed in a minimal amount of dark clothing, and using lamp black, I covered my face and arms. I had assembled in a lidded basket two thirty-foot ropes, two saws—one extra as a back-up, a small hatchet, and a knife which I fixed in my belt. My tools were simple and my plan depended on stealth.

"As captain of my ship, I was obliged to advise the officer of the deck that I intended to leave the ship on a personal matter, hoping that he alone might observe my departure. When I left my cabin I put on a hooded black rain cape that I often used in time of storms and slipped down the gangway to the waiting Whitehall rowboat tethered to the ship.

"Near Charlestown Bridge I had arranged with Billy White to have a smaller skiff waiting. I wrapped the oars of the skiff in old shirts as a muffle, pushed myself off, and rowed easily, taking care to make as little noise as possible. The wind and rain fought hard against me and the lightning, with greater frequency than I wished, lit my progress for seconds at a time. I could only hope that if I was observed from any of the ships in the harbor, I would be thought insane and consequently not worth a challenge. It took me about twenty minutes to locate the *Constitution,* but once there it was the Jackson figurehead that made it obvious I had found my target.

"I approached from the bow, the nearest point, but also the direction from which I believed I was least likely to be observed. I rowed into the shadow of the hull and secured my boat. Then I climbed soundlessly up the bobstay to the cutwater. No sentinels were outside because of the rain. I saw a further complication, however, as the aft lights of the *Independence* and *Columbus* lit up the bow of the *Constitution,* so as I worked I would be clearly visible to anyone out on this miserable night. I lay on my back on the shelter board with my basket of tools.

"I was well aware that one weakness in my plan was, having never before actually seen the figurehead, I had no idea how it might be fastened to the hull and thus how it might be detached. Once there, I had no obvious answer to my problem as I had hoped. The figure was at least life-sized and it was attached down the back from head to toe, to the hull. It would be impossible to saw down that length and probably it was attached with bolts anyway. My hatchet was too small to hack it loose, never mind the noise that would make, and it would not be enough to pry anything loose.

"I did not have a great deal of time to ponder my dilemma. So I settled for Andrew Jackson's head. It was a prominent head with long wavy white hair, high forehead, intense face, but posed in such a way that his chin was tucked back against his collar. The bolting ended at that collar so I was forced to go almost to his mouth in order to remove the head and avoid the fastening. With my well-greased hand-saw I began from the front, an awkward angle for accuracy. That angle and my suspended unstable body gave little traction to my strokes. The rain beat directly at my face, hindering my clear view of any progress. I was quickly tired but I kept sawing, aware that now I was making sounds that might well carry above the tumult of the storm. At one point I paused to rest, and having not secured my saw in any way, it slipped from me and splashed into the bay. I took out my spare with relief and considerable satisfaction, determined not to stop again.

"It took the better part of three hours to cut through the sticky southern pine. Almost through the neck, I lifted the President's head and with one swing of the hatchet, popped it loose. In grabbing for the head, I lost hatchet and saw and the three hit the water like what to me was the sound of cannon balls. I swiftly maneuvered back onto the deck of the ship. This time there was a single man on deck but I managed, by studying his patrol path, to avoid his view and scurried down the gangway into the boat.

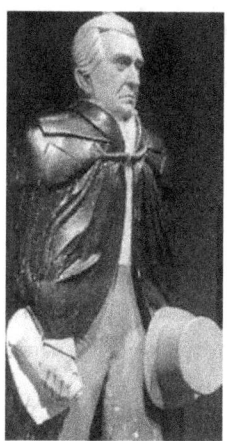

Replica of Andy Jackson figurehead

"I left no clues. I found my skiff half-filled with rain water, and as I put in my oars, heard a loud bump. There floated Andy, face up as if treading water. I brought him into the boat and rowed away from the *Constitution,* satisfied with the headless statue that graced her bow. By this time the tide was so low I had to wade a long distance just to reach shore.

"I do not know who first observed that 'Old Hickory' had been decapitated, but by afternoon the next day, all Boston had an opinion on the act and by July Fourth, the nation's patriotic celebration had been stirred to new partisanship." Samuel picked up the small wooden box and opened it for Jake.

"Is that it," asked the boy. "Is that the figurehead?"

"Well, not the real one. Of course I took only the head. This is a miniature copy of the whole figurehead made for me a few years later by a friend."

Jake peered at the figure. "It looks so stiff."

"It does. No one made any complaints when it was installed, but after I had taken the head, people took opinions on my action and the quality of the carving. Common consensus was that Laban Beecher's work was crude and stiff, but even so, most people did not see my actions as artistic criticism—rather more of a rebuke of the President.

"The Whigs, and as I said I counted myself as one of that party, were delighted and broke into cheers and drank to the health of the unknown decapitator. Democrats were outraged. I had truly made a grand entrance into politics. Commandant Elliott declared the affair an 'insult to the United States Navy, if not to the entire United States.' He offered one thousand dollars reward for the discovery of the perpetrator. When that produced no result, he threatened to court-martial all hands in Boston Yard if the vandal were not brought to charges.

"Rumors abounded, but only I knew the story and I had the head. I was euphoric about the controversy I had stirred. "I didn't rush to claim my bet from Gamaliel Pratt. He was at sea anyway at the time, but when he read the story in some newspaper somewhere in South America, he knew immediately that he owed me a quarter of his profits from his current voyage. I was aware that when I was once exposed there would be ardent cries for my dismissal as a sea captain, which I was prepared to parry with my resignation. What dramatic irony. I was a national Janus. Two faces.

"How could I generate still more legendary fame from my escapade without raising it to the rank of misdemeanor? Jake, as I retell this story I am embarrassed by how inflated my ego appears to have gotten in that time. I determined that if I took my trophy directly to President Jackson, he could not allow my punishment without encouraging ridicule, so I wrapped it in paper and scheduled the carriage ride to Washington.

"In Philadelphia on the way, I chanced upon two Whigs of my acquaintance, Willie P. Mangum from North Carolina and John Tyler from Virginia, both United States Senators. I could not resist the satisfaction to be had in telling these gentlemen, who were already aware of the much publicized decapitation of President Jackson, that I had committed the act and was now on the way to try to present my relic to the President himself.

"They saw this as perhaps the most daring political prank ever perpetrated. They drank to my health well into the evening and when we boarded the carriage for the final leg of the journey to Washington the next morning, it was as three conspirators. In Washington they stood ready to protect me from any malice from the Democrats.

"In my first attempts at access, I was unwelcome with administration officials because I would not reveal my business without assurance that I would be fully heard. I was still conscious that I was a sea captain, so I went repeatedly to the office of the Secretary of the Navy, Mahlon

Dickerson. He had been secretary only a month and was so bogged down with establishing his office that he avoided me. I knew that my father, some years before, had been acquainted with the Vice President, Martin Van Buren. I thought it had probably been during the war when father had been given his artillery command. The Vice President might not have remembered but anything was worth a try.

"I finally got my appointment, with the assistance of Senators Mangum and Tyler, and I was greeted warmly by Vice President Van Buren, who gave praise to the brave exploits of my father. I had been led to believe that he would be hostile to anything he viewed as critical to Andy Jackson. He was actually chuckling as he took my hand, and I never recall that meeting without thinking I had met a character directly out of one of Mister Charles Dickens' novels. He was roly-poly with little bantam legs and his head was flanked with fluffy earmuffs of curly white hair.

"He heard my story all the time smiling broadly. He told me he had heard much about the excitement my escapade had produced among officials in Boston. Then I opened the wrapping and rolled the President's head upon his desk. 'My God, there it is!' he cried out and began to laugh with such gusto I was startled. For just a second my mind flashed to another severed head that had landed in my lap in Sumatra. Then he assured me that the president would be amused as well and he intended to be the one who told him the story.

"First, he thought it good protocol if, as a sea captain, I presented my compliments to Secretary Dickerson. When I told him that I had tried repeatedly but unsuccessfully to do that, he offered to make the appointment for me.

"A few days later, when I was ushered into Secretary Dickerson's office, I was announced only as 'Captain Samuel Dewey of Boston.' The Secretary was a rather stuffy looking man. He had been Governor of New Jersey and a Senator and he was ill-prepared when, having met his greeting, I rolled out on his desk the severed head of his president. Dickerson threw his hands up and gasped, recognizing right away what it was and from whence it came, and scowled. Then, rapidly regaining his composure he wondered coolly, 'who, sir, are you'? I answered that I was a Cape Cod skipper named Samuel Worthington Dewey.

"Dickerson was not happy and he threatened to have me arrested. I had expected such a threat from someone in Washington, so I told him that there was no charge on which I could be held except that of trespass. On that, I would have to be tried in Middlesex County in Massachusetts where the trespass had occurred. I declared that if I was tried there and a Middlesex jury did not give me damages instead of Dickerson or even President Jackson, my name was not Dewey. It was no bluff, but perhaps un-politic out of courtesy for his office if not his person.

"I told the secretary that I would like to present the head to the president myself, considering the direct approach my best chance at redemption. He had an ironic laugh for my forwardness and said that some had called me a 'murderer.' I told him that would be difficult to prove without a body. Finally he advised me that unfortunately Jackson was then quite ill with hemorrhaging of the lungs and was not receiving any visitors. He announced stiffly that he would show the head to the president. I had the satisfaction of knowing that the vice president had beat him to it.

"Jake, I read some time later in the *Boston Globe* that when he was told, Andy Jackson 'roared' with laughter and declared 'I never did like that image. Give that man a postmaster's job!' That is how I almost became a postman. He was also reported to have said that a president should be prepared for such acts of criticism, since they came as part of politics in a free system. I found that attitude gracious in an elected officer, but I suspected that I had also severed any future I had as a sea captain. As I told you, that result I did not regret.

"Secretary Dickerson kept the head. It was not restored to the *Constitution* for more than a decade, when a new, even more stylish Greco-Roman version of Jackson was carved. A year after the incident, my friend Beecher sold his Boston studio and moved to Wisconsin. As far as I know some member of the Dickerson family must be in possession of Jackson's head to this day."

Chapter Eight

Phrenology

"Jake, I'm afraid I don't have as many treasures to show you when I describe the next part of my life." Samuel offered this confession as he continued his story with some urgency, out of concern that Jake might become obsessed with the account of his crisis in judgment in Boston. He wanted to broaden the boy's knowledge of the world and his self confidence, so he downplayed his own role in order to avoid appearing as some sort of hero in his exploits. "Nevertheless I can highlight a few of my interesting experiences that developed after the drama of stealing the president's head." He settled into his chair and began with a sequel to his story.

"Boston seemed now a place where my actions had so defined my reputation that it was impossible for me to be taken seriously, so I went to New York where I opened a brokerage business for shipping cargo. That means I negotiated contracts with manufacturers or vendors who had goods to be sent to a destination by ship. I made further contracts through my agents in foreign ports for goods to be shipped to American ports. I received payment from both directions for such transactions.

"My first office in New York was at Seventy-seven South Street. I had 'come ashore' so to speak, but had remained with the business of commerce by sea, something I had been doing already for twenty-three years. My friend, Mohammed Ali, was yet the Khedive of Egypt, but I thought I might make better use of my more recent contacts in South America and open connections with other US ports, such as New Orleans.

"There was also a family consideration that promised to present opportunities for me as a broker. My older sister, Augusta Maria, had married Frederick N. Thayer, a medical doctor. They had first settled at his home in Augusta, Maine, but Thayer took letters of introduction and moved his family to Saint Thomas, a West Indies island owned by Denmark. During the Napoleonic War, Britain for a time had taken over the island, but on its return to Danish control, the Danes developed the island as a distribution point for goods in the West Indies. The port city of Charlotte Amalie, where the Thayers located, soon had offices from German, French, British, Italian, Spanish, Sephardim, American, and Danish brokerage houses, including mine.

"The island became a pivotal point of trade for all of the Western Hemisphere and I prospered. I was particularly happy when I was in Saint Thomas, because I enjoyed getting to know again my sister whom I really left when I went to sea in eighteen twenty. She and Frederick had one son, Frederick, Junior, who was eleven, so you see I have had past experience with young men about your age.

"Another reason I liked Saint Thomas was that, unlike most of the other West Indies islands whose economies so depended on the production of sugar, Saint Thomas had few slaves. It would be another decade before the slave trade was abolished in the West Indies, but in Saint Thomas, most of the few blacks were free and they were involved with the operation of the port. Many had jobs through the brokerages. They were being educated, and some were owners of small businesses. It was a marked contrast in relationships with the other islands, and one with which I certainly felt more comfortable. Out of Saint Thomas I made many more trips to South America where I continued to add to my collection of mineral samples.

"I also had a small office in Cuba kept open for me by a Spanish friend, José eBanja. I think I was attracted to Cuba by the alternating support in the United States for the annexation of the island as a state. On the one hand I considered this a good strategic move, because of its proximity to the US, but I also came to realize that an increase in the dependence on the sugar production was going to always link Cuba to the practice of slavery.

"Unlike the United States, where slaves were never allowed to colonize based on their tribal connections in Africa, in Cuba this tribal identity had been retained. African language, worship and traditions were preserved and balanced against the high death rate associated with sugar production and the constant local rebellions against authority.

"In New York I became well acquainted with most of the men of commerce and was accepted by the business community. One strange complication was that I was not the only S.W. Dewey in business in the city down near the Battery. Solon William Dewey, advertising himself as S. W. Dewey & Company, had an office at eighty-five Water Street, as one of the larger cotton buyers. Solon Dewey's grandfather was my grandfather Benoni's brother, making us second cousins. We frequently had business dealings and on more than one occasion confusion arising over our similar names worked to our mutual advantage. Also his connections in the cotton trade gave me access to the cotton exchanges in the South, particularly in New Orleans. Cotton was the crop which drove the politics of the American South. In my later business in land speculation in the South, I found that this contact within the cotton trade was very useful.

"In eighteen thirty-five, a Scotsman named James Gordon Bennett started the *New York Herald* newspaper. He had been connected with newspapers in Boston and New York for some time and had innovative ideas about how a newspaper should be run. At that time newspapers did not go in search of news, nothing that might be called 'investigative journalism.' Instead, the practice was to wait until news broke or was suggested to the newspaper and then the newspaper would report what they heard.

"On April ten, eighteen thirty-six, a young woman named Helen Jewett was found murdered in her room at a building known to house prostitutes in lower Manhattan. James Gordon Bennett went to the scene of the crime that Sunday, examined the premises, saw the body, and interviewed the witnesses, including the woman who managed the building. The next morning the *New York Herald* printed the story in lurid detail that was not previously common in newspapers.

"The article created an instant sensation and crowds rushed to the murder scene. The other New York papers, the *Sun* and the *Transcript*, continued for a time to operate as usual in relationship to the story but soon saw their circulation plummet, so they began aggressive reporting. Not long afterward other larger newspapers throughout the country were imitating the style.

"There were many connections to the victim and the accused in Massachusetts, and so the Boston newspapers were marking all the local connections possible to the case. It was only a year and a half since these same papers were making vivid reports of my snatching of Jackson's head.

"It was reported that Helen Jewett, while a servant in the home of the father of the Chief Justice of Maine's parents in Augusta, had first become a prostitute. Such details were refuted and an entirely different scenario concerning her background came out of New England newspapers. Living in New York, I too was following the story and the New England connections interested me as well.

Murder mystery of the day

"I am certain, Jake, that after my recent notoriety, and with so many similar New England connections in time and place, it was only natural that my name would come into the business—and so it did.

"The *Herald* printed a reference to my escapades in Boston in such a way as to infer that I might have been very close to the story and therefore to the person of Helen Jewett. As a man just establishing my reputation in New York, I was incensed. Having read what I took for an insult, I stormed out the door seeking Bennett himself.

"Meeting him by happenstance on Beekman Street, I proceeded to soundly thrash the man. He was but ten years my elder so I considered it a fair fight but we were fortunately separated by bystanders. Bennett claimed then to my face that absolutely no insult had been intended and he immediately apologized for his over-zealous words and promised a correction in his paper. He seemed sincerely mortified and two days later we met at his club over drinks to further calm the conflict. As a result, James Gordon Bennett, until his death some thirty-five years later, was perhaps my truest friend and confidant in the city.

James Gordon Bennett, Sr.

"I tell you, Jake, that at the time I was the recipient of a very powerful lesson. Try never to lose control of your emotions. Most of the time cooler heads are able to accommodate differences, particularly when the conflicts are based on misinterpretations. Many a tragic mistake is made when rage takes over our actions. The old adage, 'think twice,' has sound value and is a clear sign of maturity.

"It was through the growing influence of my friend Bennett that I began to take my next steps into politics. One thing we immediately shared was a strong opposition to the administration of Andrew Jackson. Bennett quickly appreciated me because I had made the most physical expression of that dislike by chopping off the President's head. 'Nobody should do more than that,' he said.

"In the final year of his presidency, much of the dislike of Jackson was attached to his choice of successor, Martin Van Buren. You see, Jake, it is my observation that a strong president is more likely to make controversial decisions and in the process to build up enemies, often starting with single issues. The United States was then but three score years old. Our governmental form, which had never before been attempted in world history, was still evolving. The country remained divided between those who looked for a strong national government and those who sought to have stronger, more independent state governments.

"Andrew Jackson believed in a strong presidency. There were national leaders who opposed him and they gradually coalesced around a new party that they called Whigs. It took a few years for the wide range of opposition issues to become organized on a national basis, so Martin Van Buren, hand-picked by Jackson, was able to succeed him in eighteen thirty-seven.

"I already told you that my father had known Martin Van Buren, and that the vice president had eased my presentation of the Jackson head to Secretary of War Mahlon Dickerson and eventually to Andy Jackson himself. For that I recognized that I owed him some personal gratitude. In the Van Buren election, one of my Whig friends, to whom I had first divulged my actions in Boston harbor, Willie Preston Mangum, was also a candidate but he was poorly organized and his campaign did not go far. James Bennett and I debated the merits of the candidates. We agreed that neither of us was a very committed party man. In this struggle between a strong or a more fragmented government, we also agreed that we feared the potential power of a strong president. We considered that Congress had to be an equal balance against the concentration of power. There were strong leaders in Congress opposed to Jackson and we discussed the views of Henry Clay, Daniel Webster, and John C. Calhoun, among others. Unable to choose among the options, we concluded that 'the devil you know is better,' and supported Van Buren.

"President Van Buren was an experienced politician and he intended to continue for another four years the policies of Jackson. With very few tools, however, he was faced almost immediately in eighteen thirty-seven with a financial panic that defined his presidency. He refused the petition of Texas for statehood as part of a determination to keep the country out of war. It was here that Bennett and I began to turn away from support of Van Buren. We believed in the expansion of the country west toward the Pacific. We thought that position to be the destiny of the country, and we accepted the probability that expansion might very well create situations which required the country to go to war to accomplish such an aim. Bennett used the *New York Herald* to advance his positions but he always held that the newspaper was independent in its politics.

"I, on the other hand, was more directly affected by the Panic of Eighteen thirty-seven. Brokerage depended on stable markets and sound banks that could facilitate transactions. I had not been in business long enough to build a very strong fortune. I was forced to be quite conservative in my risk-taking, but I did have a strong position with my brother-in-law in Saint Thomas and reliable contacts in South America. By the end of Van Buren's single term in office, Bennett had come to believe that the president's years as a politician had made him too cautious, too prone to act with the expedient rather than to be able to seize the opportunity to press an advantage.

"Jake, I am giving you a lesson in history in the first person. It may be of use to you in your studies in school. You may be interested in knowing that I also became active in New York City politics. Look — here are some illustrations from this period." Samuel crossed the room and took from the shelf half a dozen posters which he began to unroll. "Tippecanoe and Tyler Too," he read. "That was for old General William Henry Harrison when he was elected President. Here is one about Martin Van Buren, calling him 'Martin Van Ruin.' And here is 'Old Hickory — Man of the People.'

"I am telling you about this aspect of my life in terms of my relationship with John Gordon Bennett, who was for me another example of my gravitation toward 'inquiring minds.' Remember when we first talked about that. I described it, I believe, as a person who listened in proportion to speaking and who had knowledge sufficient to the conversation. That is my memory of Bennett. I never felt I was his protégée. We brought our different experiences to discussion but in that exercise we invariably found ourselves in fundamental harmony over and over. It is a comfort to find such a relationship.

"One other subject began absorbing more of my discussions with Bennett: slavery. In that time slavery was part of almost any political, religious, or economic conversation, either in the discourse or implied by it. Slavery was defining the national discourse.

"You have heard how many times in my travels as a sea captain I had been faced with the practice of slavery around the world and how it always repelled me. In my youth, Boston had become a favored destination of slaves who successfully ran away from their masters in the

South. Then in eighteen thirty-three, the Anti-Slavery Society formed with its headquarters in New York City. My brokerage business placed me in contact with many men who had become wealthy in the slave trade. Many of the islands in the Indies and countries in South America with which I dealt still allowed the slave trade. By the end of the Van Buren Panic, I had made connections in southern cities in addition to New Orleans, particularly in the trade in tobacco and cotton, both dependent for labor on the slave.

"Jake, slavery is a moral issue. All that I had been taught in school, church, my New England home, and all my experiences in life, confirmed to me that it is wrong for one human being to own another. The only way I had seen it practiced was for one human, the master, to somehow conceive and to act to make the other less than human. Try as he might to construct Biblical justification, in the end the slave was persecuted.

"I had seen the practical side of life, however, and I understood that whole economic systems had been structured on slavery as a preferred form of labor. Remember, Jake, this was before the industrial revolution had created machines to do the work of men. The successful businessman or farmer in those societies had invested heavily in securing that labor force and to consider surrendering slavery meant bankruptcy, particularly in agriculture. I understood the dilemma my slave-owning friends faced and I saw no obvious alternative for them. I also saw how the very ownership of slaves was like a cancer of the mind for many of them. It was as if some of their own humanity had to atrophy over time.

"My personal approach to slavery was to affirm the system as a poison. I spoke against it in public discussions. I had an aversion in dealing with men who flagrantly mistreated their slaves, and to my financial detriment, I cut off doing business with them when I found such abuse. I gave money to anti-slavery causes, especially the Anti-Slavery Society. I sought out like-minded friends. I allowed myself to be numbered among the Abolitionists although I had no formal membership in any Abolitionist organization. All these things I did in order to convince my social conscience that I was doing what I could and that I was on the right side.

"Life is like that, Jake. Unless you are a saint or a martyr you self-adjust until you can tolerate your own actions. Then, I believe, most of us function until circumstances that we face demand a choice, even a risk; it is a price we will have to pay for citizenship, for being human. We may be called then to speak out, or to act out, or even to fight for a righteous belief. Even then some of us will be blinded. My conversations with James Gordon Bennett were consumed in the evolution of our beliefs in relation to slavery and we trusted each other because we were in such harmony. Isn't that funny, Jake. The man I once tried to physically thrash, had come to mean that much to my attitude toward the circumstances of my life."

Samuel had noted that Jake's face had assumed that expression of concern in his analysis of the slavery issue, which usually indicated he was conflicted by the message. It had not been his practice to anticipate the boy's confusion but to allow for the conflict to exacerbate until the lad could define it somehow himself. Now Jake spoke up. "Mr. Dewey, I think I can appreciate the struggle you had over your own views of slavery and the experiences that came to influence your opinion, but what happened when the country finally went to war over that issue?"

"Cause and effect, eh, Jake. It is a reasonable question. I have not said anything about our Civil War, and in a way that was my intention. Slavery was, of course, at the heart of the conflict. It is what differed in North and South, the thing that was the tipping point. There were other causes, most obviously economics, and there was that fundamental difference in political views between a strong central and a weak federal government. The Civil War defined winners and losers in blood, but it is not as clear that it determined right and wrong. Time and the historian usually do that. Slavery ended during the conflict but the slave as a person, had been placed at great disadvantage in relation to the national institutions, particularly in being denied good education. He is still discriminated against and may be for some time to come.

"I don't have good stories connected with that war. I didn't serve. My business was largely cut off from its market place and I did not profit from the circumstances of the war. I was separated from the South, my friends and my business connections. I had no success in maintaining any allegiance to either cause and in the end, the years of the war are more like a shadow on my life. I can put no better face upon it than that.

"I don't think that my nature was materially changed. You be the judge, but I can admit that I continued to harbor an unstable weakness for rash action and unproven theory. To the latter I can point you to Charlestown harbor. For unproven theory let me tell you about 'phrenology.'"

Samuel reached under his table behind some small boxes and pulled out a well-polished, smooth, china head like that of a manikin, the entire skull covered with transfer-print drawings of people in various attitudes from life. It appeared as a strange skull-cap, even covering the eyes. Jake had a distant look, wondering and suspicious. Samuel laughed. "Strange to see, is it not, Jake? You must wonder at the many stories I have that involve heads. I promise you that it is only co-incidental that heads figure so many times in my experiences."

"Oh, I wasn't thinking that, Mister Dewey. Is that some kind of art piece?" He was looking more closely, starting to examine the little pictures like individual puzzle pieces. "There is writing with each one. Here is one of a man lying in the street and another seems to be speaking awful roughly to him . . .'intox-i-ca-tion' it says. Here is one that seems to be a family embracing . . .'love of family.' Each picture seems to be making a point."

"Very good. You have the idea without even having been explained the source. Some people call phrenology a science. I'm afraid when I first heard of it, I thought it pure quackery. But as I did more study I began to see some value to the concept.

"The operation of our brains is little understood in our time. Phrenology focuses on personality and character and claims to be able, by examining the skull, to predict elements of character and qualities of personality. You see on this head these twenty-seven areas marked with pictures and a personality trait. Phrenology considers that by examining the bumps and indentations in the skull on an adult, and matching them to the map of the brain on this china head, that it is possible to make conclusions about strengths, weaknesses, propensities, and preferences. Phrenologists then, using their fingers and palms, can study a patient and develop a psychological profile. This is particularly useful to doctors treating all kinds of mental disorders. I think you can recognize that it is not possible to examine the brain of a living being as freely as doctors can examine and operate on the human body.

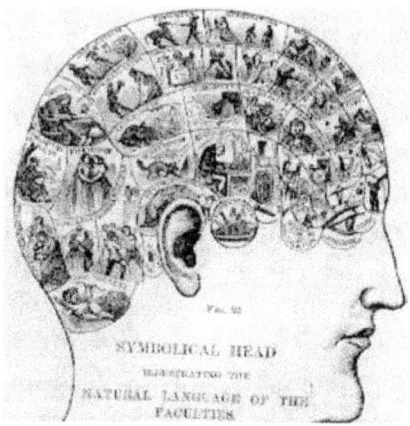

Phrenology - ceramic head

"Phrenologists say there are these numerous 'brain organs,' or functional areas, and in the human brain they are located in the same position on each person and hence under a spot on the skull. These areas include such functions as: the instinct to reproduce, to love, to be clever, to be vain, to be prideful, to remember words, to experience each of the senses, to be poetical, to be able to imitate, or to be religious. Does any of this make sense to you, Jake?"

"I guess. You mean when I grow up I will have bumps and dents on my head, under my hair that a doctor can feel and tell me if I like to fight?" All the time Jake was rubbing his head. He glanced at Samuel's head as if wondering if there might be bumps on the old man's skull. "I heard of crazy people but maybe somebody just hit them over the head and gave them a dent or a bump in the wrong place. I got a bump right here that Sidney Stuffle put there with a big stick one day when we was fighting. Wonder what it says on the head map?"

"Well, my boy, you have the general idea and you are raising some of the questions that skeptics have raised over the years. You should understand that attempts to measure the skull shape scientifically began in Germany and there have been many specialists who have spent their entire careers in the study. Here in America, Samuel Wells and the Fowler Brothers operated a phrenological business and publishing house in New York. Lorenzo Fowler was the man who actually created this phrenology head and it became famous as a symbol of the study. I knew all these men well and found them very serious and professional. Of course there were many people who attempted fame as phrenologists who were mere charlatans, who said they read heads and could mix snake oil.

"One of the more famous world authorities on phrenology came from Edinburgh, Scotland. His name was George Combe, and in eighteen thirty-eight he visited the United States on a lecture tour. I became acquainted with him and I must admit I fell under the spell of his thinking. I took part as a student in two of his classes while he was in New York and was selected for the committee that presented him with a large Grecian cup decorated with medallic portraits of five of the world leaders in this field of study including that of George Combe.

George Combe

"One of the most interesting experiences I had with Mister Combe involved the study of flat-headed American Indians. There was a tribe called by other tribes, Flathead, who lived between the Cascade Mountains and the Rocky Mountains. They were called Flatheads by other tribes that bound the heads of their children to influence their shape. The Flatheads refused to do that. Thus a confusing paradox that did confuse. Mister Combe sought to study an Indian with a flat head to determine if the binding process displaced or entirely destroyed the cerebral convolutions of the skull. At first he asked the medical officer of a fur company to take the cast of the skull of a European to his station and over time compare it with dead Flathead Indians. That was so confusing as to be bizarre.

"Then I arranged an interview with an Indian named Thomas Adams. Thomas and one other Indian with a flathead had been brought to New York by the missionary at the fur company. Mister Combe was able to examine his head and make a minute survey of the locations of his convolutions.

"Then, at my suggestion, I was able to spend a day with Thomas in New York to record my impressions of his feelings and reactions. I began by attempting to determine what thoughts he had about a deity. 'I have none,' he said. 'What about your people?' I asked him. 'No, nothing,' he responded. 'Have you not noticed growing grass that withers and dies in the winter and returns in the spring; or trees that produce fruit then lose leaves only to have more leaves and bear fruit in the spring; or have you noted the rising and setting of the sun which then rises another day?' 'We have no such thought. Nothing,' he said finally, becoming quite offended.

"We walked into a jewelry store and he observed all the shining jewelry. I asked what he would like to have. 'I would like to have it all,' he said. We went into the library room at the American Institute and when asked what he saw he would like, he said, 'I want all.'

"In many places people gave him gifts and his reaction was always to immediately stuff each in his pockets. When he then greeted someone new, his reaction was to clasp his hands over his pockets as if he feared they might take his things. He told me he liked my friends. Mister Mullen, the jeweler, presented him with a watch worth at least twenty-five dollars and he said he would put it in his trunk. I said it would be better in his pocket so he could use it to tell the time.

"We went next to a confectionary and then a grocery store. At each he said he wanted all. He was given gifts in each but he said he had no wish to share anything with William—the other Indian who traveled with him. He wanted to put everything in his trunk. He said he wanted clothes and I said he would soon have money enough of his own to buy what he wanted. He said he did not want to buy clothes; he wanted my friends to give him clothes. He had not been long in town, but whenever we went out anywhere, he would point and say 'my house is there.' Even when I tried to lose him by taking unfamiliar routes, he could always point to where his house was.

"When we did return to his house, I was left standing in the attic hall while he rushed in and secured all his presents in his trunk. He resisted my request to see William, I think because he thought somehow it might alter my willingness to get him presents. He claimed that William was asleep but I could see his eyes open and William showed real jealousy that Thomas had gotten so many gifts.

"When I talked with William I found him superior in every way to Thomas. He spoke directly to each of my questions. Thomas showed no concern for his friend's health, seeming to fear the time when he could again get out. Thomas kept pulling my sleeve as I talked with William, showing me that William had brought much bigger trunks. 'He got three trunks,' he said. As I parted with them, Thomas was still on the subject of the trunks.

"I asked them both about a deity. Together they said that they knew there was God and that they prayed to God. Thomas said that when he returned to the tribe he intended to convert them all to Christians. He said that before the missionaries came they frequently killed each other but the missionaries told them it was wrong to kill, and if they did, they would be hanged. They said they did not like to be hanged so they no longer killed. He said he wanted to live a long life.

"On still another occasion I was with Thomas at a Methodist Church meeting and Mister Lee, the missionary who had brought him here, was speaking. I watched Thomas as Mister Lee spoke about how the Flatheads had converted to Christianity. After the program I attempted again to question Thomas on the subject of his beliefs and he resisted. Then I put a silver piece in his hand and he became so talkative that I could hardly keep up with him.

"Some time before they were to return home in November, William died and I went to the funeral, which was open to the public. I sat with Thomas right in line between me and the corpse so I could watch Thomas's reactions. The service lasted two hours and during the whole time, even during the most emotional passages, Thomas showed no visible reaction. Afterwards I took his hand, as he was to be the chief mourner, and we followed the hearse for an hour and a half to the cemetery with about a thousand others. During the long trip, delayed several times by the size of the following, he was still stoic except when he told me he was wearing William's coat and it did not fit him. Could I get one of my friends to give him a better coat?

"Mister Combe was very disturbed that the doctor who had treated William, who also had on occasion ridiculed phrenology, had not taken any measurement data from the corpse before the burial. His point was that even when there were professional disagreements in the medical field, every doctor should be willing and anxious to assemble information that might be of value to another man's research."

"Do you still believe in bumps, Mister Dewey?"

Samuel gave a pensive nod. "I am convinced still that the brain is somehow functionally divided. I think we have learned enough medically from the mere observation of people who have had brain injuries, that the effects of those blows depend on exactly where on the brain there was impact. To the extent that function and personality are surely linked, it seems plausible still that a brain has a 'map.' I do not, however, hold with the readings of the bumps and dents of the skull.

"I realize that a technical discussion such as this is a challenge for you to understand. It is through study that science and medicine, sailing ships and commerce, geology and mineralogy, and even what we today call political science, are advanced. Never be afraid of more learning.

"It is necessary to believe passionately in an incomplete theory in order to somehow push through to the truth. Don't be afraid to be wrong. At the same time be alert and prepared to test every side objectively. As you grow older you will find that is more difficult because in absorbing knowledge, humans also assume prejudices."

"It's hard to get older, isn't it, Mister Dewey?"

"But, Jake, the struggle is half the fun. Some people try to be children all their lives because they are afraid of the struggle of growing up."

"Oh, I'm ready to grow up, Mister Dewey. I'm not really sure that I will want to go away to sea when I am thirteen, but I am ready to be a man."

After Jake went home, Samuel thought about the boy as an adult. If he could finger Jake's grown up head, what characteristics would he expect to observe? Well, certainly empathy. He saw it as unusual that an eleven-year-old boy was willing to spend time with Samuel Dewey. But Jake heard these stories with not just empathy but with marvel. The boy was sensitive to his surroundings. He never presumed or took advantage—respecting everything. Jake also displayed a mischievous mind, not a mean spirit, but expansive and energetic.

The next day Samuel had, on his desk, a shiny copper plate inscribed "Samuel Wetherill, Philadelphia." On the back, in his handwriting, Samuel Dewey had recorded, "the First manufacturer of Velverets, Jeans, Fustians and other cloths in America used by him as early as 1782 to print Cards and Labels for his manufacturers."

"Jake, this relic was given to me by Samuel Wetherill, Junior, my friend from Philadelphia and a member of a family of generations of 'inquiring minds.' It often happens that an ancestor, in an early generation of a family, will make a discovery or become active in a business, and will pass on that passion of interest to several succeeding generations. If the earlier family member established a fortune in his invention or business, later generations stay involved simply because they own so much stock, or inherited such a sizeable interest, that they cannot ignore the business even if they wanted to.

"The Wetherill family was somewhat different in that in each succeeding generation their work improved on the initial inventiveness of the original Samuel Wetherill. He was a Quaker, and you know that Pennsylvania was founded by Quakers, a society of believers who held membership in the faith to a very high standard of social commitment. Quakers were opposed to war and any members who would take up the sword were 'disowned,' meaning their names were taken off the roll and the Quakers had nothing further to do with them.

"Samuel began as a carpenter and house builder. Then, like my notes on the copper plate say, he entered the weaving business and produced the first of a number of types of fabric in America. He needed dyes for his fabric and, because dyes had to be imported, he began to make his own chemicals. That led him to be the first in America to make white lead, used for years in paint as the principle source of white. The process was to cast or mold metallic lead in small 'buckles' which were then corroded with acid and carbon dioxide. Then the buckles were placed in a pot of vinegar—acetic acid—in stacks and left for six to fourteen weeks. By that time the blue-grey lead had corroded the buckles. The buckles were scraped and pounded to remove the white lead, which was then shipped in powder form. This was in particular demand, because at that time, hulls and floors of Navy ships were painted with white lead paint regularly to waterproof the timbers and limit infestation of worms.

Wetherhill & Brother - Philadelphia

"During the Revolutionary War, old Samuel Wetherill refused to follow Quaker practice and he became active on the Patriot side, providing cloth for General Washington's Army. The Quakers disowned him and several other Quakers who also took sides. These men had joined together in the defense of Philadelphia and later founded the Society of Free Quakers, sometimes called the 'Fighting Quakers.'

"During the War of Eighteen Twelve, this same man undersold his fabric production to destroy the foreign importation of cloth. This inventive spirit combined with a willingness to see business opportunities and take commercial advantage, was passed to the later generations of his family.

"His sons, particularly Samuel Junior, expanded his chemical business. The demand for white lead exceeded their processing capacity, and this Samuel was driven to develop zinc oxide as a less expensive and non-toxic substitute for white lead. He mixed the ore with anthracite coal and heated it to make his zinc oxide. Then he founded his own factory on the Lehigh River. Later he created the first ingots of spelter, a pure metallic zinc, for which he obtained a patent. During the Civil War this process accounted for the manufacture of buttons, belt buckles, rifle cartridges, weapons parts, and finally souvenirs of the conflict.

"His son, John Price Wetherill, became Vice President of the Academy of Sciences in Philadelphia. I was well acquainted with him and his father through my interest in minerals and I helped put together several New York capitalists, whose investment financed the establishment of the Pennsylvania and Lehigh Zinc Company. Samuel the Second presented me this copper plate as a memento of our friendship, knowing that I admired the work of this founding family of industry.

"Here you have an example of a family whose accomplishments, motivating from within, inspired generations of creativity. That is not easy. There is a saying, 'pauper to pauper in three generations,' that makes fun of the many cases where a man, born into poverty, worked hard, accomplished a great deal, and in the process made a fortune. Then his son grew up lazy, spent the fortune and the grandson was back in poverty. Money is not the most important thing that you can leave to your children. Without good character, a good education, and common sense, they can come to nothingness."

Samuel observed that Jake had listened closely. "You may wonder Jake, if I have told you these stories as completely as you would like, or that I have told you as much as you would want. Is that right?"

"Well, maybe so, Mister Dewey, but I can see that there is a message in these stories if I can remember all that you have told me."

"You have certainly been given a lot of information. What I hope is that at times you will be able to match the details of one of the stories to some circumstance you might encounter and thereby help you in making the right decision. By that I mean when you discover you must choose between what is right or wrong, or if you have only two not so good choices, you will choose the better one."

"Mister Dewey, I can see the kind of people that you admire. I see as well that you generally have a friendly attitude to most people. What I would also like to know is how you can tell when you have a good friend."

"My boy, friendship is not a science. It is a quality of life that can serve a person well. Some people are so introverted, so turned into themselves, that they don't allow anyone to be their friend. They consider it too big a risk. To lose a friend, or worse, to be betrayed by a friend, can be devastating. It is like a death. But we know that death is part of life and life is more fulfilled if we risk making friendships.

"If you asked many people about their friends, they might list a few as 'good friends' and some as just 'regular friends.' I might answer you that I have had about six close friends in my life. These are people with whom I felt comfortable in sharing my thoughts, my fears, and my ambitions. I do not always agree with my friends. We don't just think alike but we approach thought in very much the same way.

"We hear our friends out. We show respect for their opinions. We love the warmth of being in their presence. But we can share the quality of friendship beyond our close friends. Remember when you meet someone, that you are sharing your space and time with them, like it or not. It is better for your health and safety that sharing time is not confrontational. That is why it is usually better to be friendly as your contribution to the shared space. If that is not possible, try to avoid precipitous acts, but be on guard."

A day or two later, Jake came across a carved sign inscribed, "The Sunrise."

"I'll bet this is some kind of nameplate," speculated Jake. "Is it the name of one of your sailing ships, Mister Dewey?"

"Another good guess, Jake. You are getting a real feel for my collection, which means you must be listening. That is the nameplate from a ship but it is from a canal boat, and I must admit it represents one of my less profitable business adventures.

"Remember when I told you about packet boats, sailboats that were beginning to use steam and were establishing scheduled sailings between Europe and the United States? "

"I remember that your first command was a packet boat and it was called...," there was a long pause as Jake looked down, bunching his lips to one side; then he looked up with a bright smile and a snap of his fingers, "...the *Messenger*. And you loved that ship."

"Right on all counts, Jake. Well, the application of steam to sailing ships was also applied to smaller river boats and canal boats. You have heard of the Chesapeake and Ohio Canal. It runs from Cumberland, Maryland to Washington, DC. You may not know that George Washington was one of the earlier promoters of this canal. He saw it as a way to connect the Eastern Seaboard with the Great Lakes and the Ohio River.

"Most men of vision saw that if our new country was to advance to its full potential, it was necessary that we have lines of communication and commerce over vast areas. At first that could only be accomplished using rivers, and the use of rivers was later supplemented by the difficult efforts to build roads. East of the Mississippi, the Appalachian Mountains defined the river flow: east of the mountains to the Atlantic Ocean and west to the Mississippi and the Gulf of Mexico. The Erie Canal had created a connection from Lake Erie to the Atlantic Ocean via the Hudson River. From our new capital city, the Chesapeake and Ohio Canal sought a similar connection with the Ohio River. They started with the work that George Washington's Potomac Company had done to make that river more navigable. That had been done by deepening the river channel and by cutting skirting channels around the impassible rapids in the river. The Chesapeake and Ohio Canal was finally built as a separate canal paralleling the river.

Chesapeake & Ohio Canal

"Using the same logic that had established the Atlantic steam packet service, I applied for and received the first contract for such a service on the C&O Canal. Earlier there had been prohibitions against using steam on the canal, but when it was finally approved, the Directors had to build in an incentive to make steam packets attractive.

"Terms of my arrangement stated the boats had to travel at a minimum of eight miles per hour. There was always a difference of opinion over whether the higher speed of the steam packets, thus their wake, did excessive damage to the berm of the canal. By eighteen sixty, the canal company had again banned the use of steam on the canal.

"My canal project saw little profit because it was not yet possible to integrate the freight moved on the canal very well with sea cargo, which had been my vision. It is also true that the almost simultaneous development of the Baltimore and Ohio Railroad and the Winchester and Potomac Railroad contradicted the value of the canal. Railroads were soon found to be more profitable than canals to build and maintain, and in many ways served the same function in commerce. I then turned my attention to the encouragement of railroads, although my interest in the Chesapeake and Ohio Canal had introduced me to more of the visionaries in the commercial development of the country."

Chapter Nine

Dewey Diamond

"You remember before we talked about the precious stones of South America I introduced you to all the minerals that I collected in North Carolina in the Sauratown Mountains?"

"Yes," Jake said, beaming. "They are in that box over there with the 'wiggly grit.'"

"Well, let me start there to tell you about the largest diamond ever found in North America." Jake looked up, ready to go, obviously fascinated with the idea of this story.

"Get me the wiggly grit." Samuel said, smiling at Jake's delight and pointing.

Jake fumbled in the box by the side of the open closet. He identified the sandy, brown rock right away and handed it to Samuel.

"I think I had planned to tell you this story much earlier, but as I recall we got off on stories of the sea. Do you remember what the real name for this rock was, Jake?"

"Ita--- Ita --- something, I think.

"Itacolumite. And do you remember that I said that Doctor Pepper, when he first showed me that rock, had said it was reported that where this rock was found, in South America and some place in Russia, it was presumed likely that one could also find diamonds?"

"Is that where you found the big diamond, Mister Dewey?"

"No. Now slow down, Jake. I was just giving you some reference points. This story does start then, when I was spending so much time in North Carolina, along the Dan and Yadkin Rivers, and I was operating out of a land office in Danville. It was in May of eighteen fifty-four that someone showed me a copy of the *Richmond Penny Post* that contained a strange story.

"It seemed a laborer named Benjamin Moore, and several others were leveling a small hill of dirt at the northwest corner of Ninth and Perry Streets in the part near the town that locals called Manchester. That area across the James River from Richmond has since become part of that city.

One of the men dug up what he saw as a shiny rock and tossed it to the side. Benjamin Moore took a closer look.

"The stone was about the size of a chestnut, and that night he took it home to show his six children. There he cleaned it and the children thought it very pretty. So they made it part of their game of pickups. One day, Moore's boss, James Fisher, was visiting the home and saw the children at play and asked about their special rock. Fisher suggested that Moore should take the rock to a jeweler as he might have something of value. Here is what he had." Samuel was standing at the closet and brought out a chestnut-sized rock.

"Is that it?" Jake's eyes shot wide open. His voice rose as he pointed at the stone. "Is that the diamond you found?"

"It is a replica of what he found, Jake. It looks just like it. Benjamin Moore took the rock to the jewelry shop of Tyler & Mitchell, and Mister John H. Tyler concluded that it was indeed a twenty-eight and three quarter carat diamond. It was given the name, the 'Manchester Diamond.' The *Penny Post*, in telling the story, had a lot of nonsense about tests made to prove it was a diamond. I was intrigued, and thought that I had more experience with testing gemstones than most, so I went to Richmond. By this time the paper had declared the stone worth a place in any curiosity cabinet in the world and it would be a conspicuous ornament in the richest imperial crown.

"You can imagine how much interest and rumor had already surfaced by the time I arrived to visit Mr. Moore and to examine the diamond. You can see that it has no sharp angles but four protruding points at the apex of the angles. I had it placed in a small iron furnace for about two hours and found it uninjured and brighter than ever when brought out. I was convinced that it was a diamond.

"The jeweler, Mr. Tyler, pronounced it to have a value of four thousand dollars. I negotiated with Mister Moore, first offering to take the stone to New York for appraisal, at which time I would give him half the appraised value. He seemed reluctant to allow it now to go out of his hands but he badly needed cash, so I agreed to pay him fifteen hundred dollars for the diamond. I was taking a risk, because although I was certain it was a diamond, it had imperfections, and from a scientific standpoint, there was the obvious question of how it came to be found in a street in Richmond, Virginia.

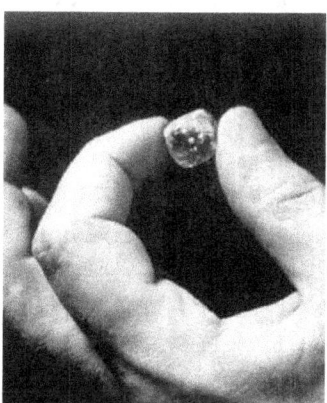

Dewey Diamond

"Much later it was concluded that it may have originated from the Mount Horeb kimberlite of Rockbridge County—that is in the same James River drainage basin—and over millennia it could have washed down the river. I had no way of knowing that possibility then and many people suspected some kind of chicanery associated with the stone's discovery. Later still, the story circulated in Richmond that I had swindled Benjamin Moore, taken the stone and never paid him for it. I guess that such tales were inevitable.

"I took the stone with great secrecy by coach to New York and when the first newspaper report surfaced there, it was called the 'Dewey Diamond.' Now it was described as an octahedron with slightly rounded faces and a large flaw on one side, a faint greenish-white in color with perfect transparency. I took it to be seen by all the people in New York whom I considered to have some expertise with the study of gems. The vast majority agreed that it was not a perfect diamond, but that in Europe it might be cut and would yield a very large diamond.

"For almost fifteen years, I was the owner of the Dewey Diamond. What doors had not been open to me by my fame for sawing off the head of Andrew Jackson were now open to me as a serious geologist and mineralogist and owner of this excessively valuable diamond. Wouldn't my friend the Khedive of Egypt have been impressed? I was sought after in society circles in New York and Boston. I thought it appropriate to give the gem an extravagant name and so called it the *Ominoor,* or 'Son of Light.' I placed it on display at Ball, Black & Company where it was a sensational attraction.

"My friend John Gordon Bennett was amused about the attention I was getting for possessing this stone, saying, 'You are a man of diverse affairs: owner of the Dewey Diamond and Abolitionist.' At first I made light of his judgment, but as time passed, I too found that the scope of my interests gave a false impression of my own means and success.

"Jake, I was really trapped between my ego and my moral integrity. I liked my access to power, the doors that were open. My opinion carried weight and I believed I had earned that esteem. But I could feel the attention seeping into my character and taking hold.

"It was clear that, as a nation, we approached war. From a legal and political standpoint it was the struggle between Federalists and the state governments, but the catalyst, the fuse, was slavery. My connections in the South and the North gave me to believe that I could be a force to hold back the inevitable. Even after John Brown's Raid at Harpers Ferry, I wrote to Henry Wise, Governor of Virginia, urging him to take steps toward freeing the slaves. He had to recognize that the opinion of the vast majority in the North, far beyond those who identified themselves as Abolitionists, opposed the continuation of slavery. I told him flatly that 'all of us at the North sympathize with the Martyr of Harpers Ferry.'

"Barrett and I supported Abraham Lincoln in eighteen sixty, just as many in the South used his election as the final perceived indignity that drove them to secession. I saw my country shattered by the final lunacy, unable to cure itself. I struggled with hollow success. Do you know what that means, Jake?"

Jake squirmed in his chair, knit his eyebrows, "I am having a hard time, Mister Dewey. I can tell this is difficult for you to talk about, but I think you want to tell me something or impress me with some message. I am not sure what it is."

"You are a young man. You have not lived long enough to have experienced substantial disappointment in any of your actions. I do not want you to think from my stories that I have lived without such disappointments, or that life is a series of exciting experiences where you are always the hero. We are human and I have told you of several times when I have fallen short, when I think about my own expectations for myself. The difference here, in this part of my life that I am telling you about, is that I was influenced by my fame to see it as success and I was finding it hollow. A reputation built solely on fame can be very unfulfilling, Jake. Shakespeare called it 'vaulting ambition, which o'erleaps itself and falls on the other side.' I was positioned as a sea captain, a folk hero, a recognized professional, possessor of an object many others coveted, and a vocal advocate of social reform, to accomplish considerable acts of substance in my life.

"Alas, I must admit to you that was not the course of my remaining years. What I am saying to you, lad, is that your life is the sum of all its parts, not just the exciting or more provocative, neither just the trials nor the disappointments. I do not now regret my life or my actions. I am at an age where I can recognize opportunities missed and potential, unfulfilled. That is the blessing and the curse of old age. So let's talk more about diamonds."

Samuel had gotten more prophetic than he had intended with Jake. Another curse of old age, he groused internally — the wish to talk and the unwillingness to gauge the patience or the maturity of the audience.

"At the end of the war, slavery was abandoned, but the price had been horrible: death and destruction and the economic ruin of the Southern states where I had intended to build my economic success. And yet, all was not lost for me. In New York, Boston and Philadelphia, my friends survived the war rich and victorious. We had a nation to rebuild and we had control of the instruments of reconstruction.

"Although my talents were not in high demand as part of the war effort, I had a solid base for post-war speculation. I found that the ownership of the Dewey Diamond made credit available to me in almost unquestioned amounts. I made investments in stock and land and buildings. I was asked to be an investor in some very promising corporations, in railroad projects. My knowledge of minerals was in demand, as wealth bred the appetite for the ornaments of riches. I knew where precious gems had been found in the world. The famous jewelry houses were in Paris, London, Saint Petersburg, Amsterdam, and

Rotterdam, but there were good jewelry houses in New York and Philadelphia as well.

"One of the better jewelers in Boston was Henry D. Morse. In eighteen sixty-one, he was the first American to turn his attention to diamond cutting. All the best diamond cutters were in Holland, so he brought Dutch diamond cutters over to teach his American apprentices. He of course knew about the Dewey Diamond, and we began to discuss cutting this raw diamond in order to produce the largest and finest gems possible. I had exact replicas of the uncut stone made, one each for the U.S. Mint in Philadelphia, Peabody Museum in New Haven, Connecticut, Field Museum of Natural History in Chicago, the Smithsonian, and for myself. Mister Morse knew that if he made a successful cut of the diamond, he would establish his reputation in America. We eventually agreed that I would pay him fifteen hundred dollars to cut the Dewey Diamond into a stone of about twelve carats with some ancillary smaller diamonds. In the spring of eighteen sixty-nine, Morse succeeded in making a cut diamond of eleven point sixty- nine carats. Unfortunately," Samuel lowered his head and wagged it with a sigh, "the gem proved off-color and imperfect and was worth less than I had paid to have it cut.

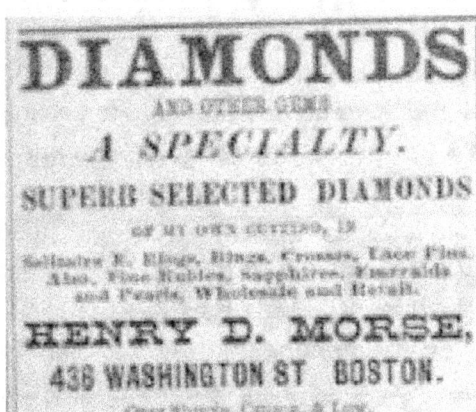

Morse Advertisement

"I was devastated. I had lost money on the original purchase *and* the cutting. I had also lost the borrowing power I had enjoyed in the uncut stone, and in the process, a good bit of fame." Samuel paused with a reflective frown, head down and chin cradled between a forefinger and thumb. "I was soon to find out that my losses had only begun." He sighed, then went on.

"In spite of the Gold Rush before the war, gold was scarce in America. A Gold Exchange had been formed in eighteen sixty-four, encouraged by the highly speculative business in precious metals. The Exchange office was in New York, and because of my reputation in the field of geology, I was constantly in discussions with investors of all consequence about the fluctuating value of gold. There were concerns about the Stock Exchange, which at that time was being manipulated by various capitalists in connection with larger railroads.

"On September twenty-four, eighteen sixty-nine, speculators led by Jim Fisk and Jay Gould attempted to corner the market on gold and run up the price. That day came to be called 'Black Friday'. They ran the price per ounce up from one forty-seven to one sixty-three. President Grant's Administration put four million in gold onto the market and in fifteen minutes the price was driven back to one forty-seven. Many investors were ruined. Wall Street brokerage houses failed. I was a minor player, not a speculator, but because I had not anticipated the assault on the gold market, my reputation was weakened.

"Jake, I know that all this talk about stock markets and gold exchanges may be difficult to follow, but it is the only way I can discuss this part of my life. I had been one of the people whom others said made fortunes in the stock and commodities markets. In my case that was an exaggeration. For a while I did make considerable profit. I was knowledgeable about investments and my trade in land was active again. Nonetheless, disappointments over the value of the Dewey Diamond, followed so soon by Black Friday, placed me in a very vulnerable position.

Panic of 1873 - *Leslie's Illustrated*

"Then, just four years later, came the Panic of eighteen seventy-three, precipitated by the failure of the large and respected banking house, Jay Cooke and Company. The Stock Exchange closed for ten days. The brokers were thunderstruck for a moment, then there was a run on the banks. Some insiders had been informed of the pending doom and were ahead of the rush. I was at the Exchange. There was an explosion as brokers tumbled pell-mell over each other to reach their respective offices and preserve what they could. I never completely recovered from these waves of disappointments. In the middle of all this misadventure, my friend, James Gordon Bennett, died. After the cutting of the stone in eighteen sixty-nine, I had given Bennett a ring made from one of the finer stones from the Dewey Diamond as a demonstration of my high regard for that gentleman.

"The story of the eleven-carat stone is more bizarre. I mortgaged the stone to John Anglist, and when I was so affected by the panic, I was unable to redeem it. That gentleman then mortgaged it for six thousand dollars to John Morrissey, one of the true characters of our age. Some people have said that I sold the diamond to Morrissey for sixteen thousand but that is just not true.

"Morrissey was born in Tipperary, Ireland and came as a child with his parents to Troy, New York. He soon went to work for an Irish crime boss and by the time he was eighteen, he had been indicted twice for burglary, once for assault and battery, and once for assault with intent to kill. He also showed a driving ambition, and while working as a bouncer in a brothel in South Troy, taught himself to read and write.

"During a fight with another gang member, he was pinned on his back on some burning coals. He endured the pain of his burning flesh, became enraged and beat the other man senseless while smoke from his own burning skin rose from his back. With that he got his nickname, 'Old Smoke.' He went to California during the Gold Rush where he made a fortune as a gambler and became a professional prizefighter.

Congressman John Morrissey, 1867-1871

"Morrissey returned to New York and he repeatedly challenged James Ambrose 'Yankee' Sullivan, at that time considered the American Champion of Prizefighting—which was an illegal sport in most places. They finally met at Boston Corner. Sullivan carried most of the fight but Morrissey held his own. In the thirty-seventh round, a riot broke out when Sullivan struck Morrissey while the latter was on his knees. Morrissey stayed out of the brawl as crowds jumped into the ring. The referee awarded the fight to Morrissey and he became an Irish hero.

"Next he became involved in New York politics as a kind of strong man, and a rivalry developed with 'Billy the Butcher' Poole, an enforcer for the Know-Nothing Party, leader of the 'Bowery Boys' and a boxer. Morrissey was hired to prevent Poole and his gang from smashing the ballot boxes and frightening away the voters. Morrissey's gang was the 'Dead Rabbits.'

"They succeeded to the extent that Tammany Hall gave Morrissey a license to open a gambling house with police protection. A year later, eighteen fifty-five, Morrissey lost a bare-knuckle fight to 'Billy the Butcher.' Afterwards, one of Morrissey's men, named Evans, shot and mortally wounded Poole in a saloon on Broadway. Both Evans and Morrissey were indicted, but were released after three trials all ended in hung juries. Morrissey held the Bare-Knuckle Heavyweight Championship until eighteen fifty-nine, when his wife finally persuaded him to retire.

"He established a successful gambling house at Saratoga Springs in New York and proved his vision in establishing, along with William Travers, John Hunter, and Leonard Jerome, the Saratoga Race Track and 'The Club House,' a casino. They attracted the likes of three presidents: Hayes, Arthur and Ulysses Grant, along with other notables such as Cornelius Vanderbilt, John D. Rockefeller and Mark Twain. He added a hotel, health spa, opera house, theater, and elegant ballrooms. At one time he owned an interest in sixteen casinos, five in New York City.

Heavyweight boxing champion - 1853-1857 - John Morrissey

"He became one of the wealthiest people in America. Then, with the backing of Tammany, he ran for Congress and twice won a seat. He became well-known for his strong-armed tactics and his claim that he could 'lick any man in the House'—meaning, of course, the House of Representatives," Samuel explained.

Sarasota Springs - America's first gambling resort

"About this time he made a loan of six thousand dollars to John Anglist, who used the Dewey Diamond as collateral. When Anglist could not repay, Morrissey became the owner of the Dewey Diamond, which immediately became known as the 'Morrissey Diamond.' I have heard it said that one night he appeared with his wife at the casino at Saratoga Springs—she wearing thirty-five thousand dollars worth of diamonds, and he wearing the Morrissey Diamond in a ring on his finger.

"Jake, a less than bitter ending should be put to the story of the Dewey Diamond. A few years later, while walking in a field in New Jersey as a geologist, I picked up the largest ruby ever found in America. This gave me a reprieve of my reputation as a geologist and the sale of the ruby put my finances back in order. It seemed anti-climactic as if, after all those years, I was provided something for my old age.

"You have been a marvelous audience for my rambling, Jake. I cannot think of a gift I would prize more. I have thought much of life as a coming and going. We come into this life with nothing and we will leave it the same way. The measure of life seems to me to be what we do with what we are given. I have my treasures as my biography. When I am gone I have arranged that they go to the Philadelphia Natural History Museum."

"Mister Dewey, this sounds so final. Are you saying that I should not come again? Are the stories over?"

"I don't think we should put it that way, Jake. We will see each other each day at *Fiddler's Rest,* and you are always welcome here in this room. You have let an old man speak of his past, and I believe that you truly enjoyed hearing what I said. You are too young to know what a gift that has been to me. I trust that what I have said has opened in you a joyful anticipation of what life can be. We will continue to talk as long as our conversations give you pleasure. Is that a fair bargain?"

Chapter Ten

Hero of Manila Bay

"Mister Dewey! Mister Dewey!" Jake's voice became clearer as he ran across the street toward the door to the stairs. He tugged at the door frantically against the strong wind. It sprang open to his effort. "Mister Dewey," he yelled from the top of the stairs. "*The Inquirer* calls him the 'Hero of Manila!' Look here, Mister Dewey!"

"Lad, calm yourself. What is the cause of such a fuss?"

"Look here, Mister Dewey," he kept saying.

Dewey looked at the front page. "Dewey sinks Spanish Fleet," he read aloud. "Admiral is Hero of Manila." Then he continued to read:

"When the United States declared war on Spain on April twenty-five, eighteen ninety-eight, Admiral George Dewey, commander of the Asiatic Fleet of the U. S. Navy, was in the port of Hong Kong. The following day he received orders to 'capture or destroy the Spanish Squadron,' then believed to be based in Manila, Philippines. His fleet arrived in Manila Bay and on May first, he is said to have given the order to the captain of his flagship, 'You may fire when ready, Gridley.' Within six hours his fleet had sunk or captured the entire Spanish Pacific fleet under Admiral Patricio Montojo y Pasaron and destroyed all Manila shore batteries. He forcefully defeated an attempt by German naval vessels in the bay to interfere with his operations. In the entire battle he lost only a single man and had only eight wounded. Hurrah for old George."

Admiral George W. Dewey

"Didn't you say he was your cousin, Mister Dewey? He is a hero just like you—a sea captain."

"We are indeed related, Jake, but I dare say he will be far the greater 'hero,' as you put it. Again, we go back to Benoni, my grandfather. He had a brother, William Dewey, who was the great-grandfather of Admiral Dewey. I have met the Admiral, when he was a young man, but I knew his father, Doctor Julius Yemans Dewey, very well. They lived in Berlin, Vermont." Dewey shook his head in disbelief. "Can you believe it, Jake?"

"Mister Dewey, do you suppose Admiral Dewey will put the head of Admiral Pasaron on President McKinley's desk?"

* * *

Photograph of Samuel W. Dewey

Samuel Worthington Dewey died June 9, 1899 in Philadelphia.

The New York Times began his obituary, "PHILADELPHIA. June 10. Capt. Samuel Dewey, a cousin of the Admiral, and one of the most picturesque characters in American history, died Friday afternoon in a tenement house on Cherry Street, near Sixth Street. Captain Dewey was ninety-three years old, and his death is assigned to senile debility. He died poor and alone, and few knew that the man who made himself famous during President Jackson's Administration, by cutting off the figurehead of the President from the frigate *Constitution*, has been living for months past in a cheap furnished-room house."

Epilogue

In most cases in this novel I have used documented incidents from the life of Samuel W. Dewey and have imagined the interplay between Dewey and the young boy, Jake. The exception to that policy was Dewey's experiences while a sea captain. Although I know where he sailed during the various periods and I know the ships on which he sailed, I have no record of his exploits. Therefore I made a study of the times and common experiences of sailors and created incidents for Dewey. I tried to be very faithful to the research and to the nature of Samuel Dewey's interests.

In subsequent years the Dewey Diamond was further cut and disbursed. The only clues to the present whereabouts of the main stone are through John Morrissey and a single reference I found, that when he died it went into the possession of Alvin Adams of the Adams Express Company. This information is confusing at best, because Morrissey died in 1878 and Alvin Adams died in 1877. In the text I have noted the locations where glass copies were placed.

The path of ownership of the head and body of the figurehead of President Andrew Jackson from the USS Constitution is a story ultimately with closure. The decapitated body block was replaced for a time on the bow of the USS Constitution by a full replica of the original, but eventually was removed altogether. In 1936 the original body of the figurehead surfaced in the Museum of the City of New York. Meanwhile the head was kept for a time by the family of Secretary of the Navy, Mahlon Dickerson. Then it was reported to be in a Massachusetts amusement park, a museum in Newark, NJ, with a woman in Brooklyn, and in France. It was recovered in 1996 and was re-united with the body at the Museum of the City of New York. The article in the New York Times, September 22, 2009, was a reference to this return.

A recent segment of the NPR series, History Detectives, featured a piece of rough cut wood about six inches square. A note with the relic said it was chopped from the figurehead of Andrew Jackson that had once adorned the USS Constitution. On the program, the researcher was led to the Museum of the City of New York and was told the head of the

Jackson figurehead had only recently been returned. When presented, the block of wood fit perfectly into the space between the head and body, confirming that it must have been chopped out by workmen when removing the headless statue after the 1839 beheading.

Finally, the body of Samuel Worthington Dewey himself is found in the Silverbrook Section of Arlington National Cemetery, eligible for burial there through his service in the US Navy. It seems appropriate that this man, "one of the most picturesque characters in American history," should find permanent rest among our national heroes.

Ryan Ray Rodenbough

As I wrote this book, I also had days of the week when I picked up my grandson, Ryan, from Greensboro Day School and kept him until one of his parents, who were both doctors, could pick him up. As I wrote it, I planned to start reading the book to him on Fridays because that was the day he typically did not have homework. Coming home in the car from school that first Friday, I began setting up the method I had planned to use while writing the book. I had already asked him the week before if he wanted to write a book with me and he had given his typical enthusiastic answer of limited conviction, "Sure!" I wasn't so sure but I was determined to be flexible. This would not be boring or it would make no sense. I wasn't doing this for me. I was doing it for us. I already had plans to write a non-fiction version of Samuel Worthington Dewey's life. This would be our book, based on the life of Samuel Dewey.

To Ryan, what I was proposing was less than a mystery but more than an understood concept. He seemed more than willing to give it a good try. As we drove, I set the scene, particularly of the first chapter. When we arrived at home he put down his book pack and his computer and gave our Beagle/Jack Russell, Katie, a full dose of loving and a romp up the hall and around the living room.

I suggested we could go back in my office and I would begin with reading the first chapter. We got settled, he in the Kennedy rocker and I at my desk. We talked some more. Then I showed him the first two chapters of "our book" in a white spiral binder. I had him read the title page, "Stealing Andrew Jackson's Head, a Novel based on the life of Captain S. W. Dewey, by Charles D. Rodenbough." Then I pointed at the bottom of the title page, "Technical Consultant: Ryan Ray Rodenbough." He looked up and said softly, "Wow."

"Ryan," I said, "I am not just giving that credit to you. You are going to have to earn it. You see, I know how an old man thinks, what interests him. I don't know for certain how a young person thinks. Oh, I was young once and I have my idea about how you might think, but I have to use memory, and memory is not always as reliable as it might be. As you hear this book, I need you to comment, to consider, to tell me when you don't understand. In this case I am not writing a book for young people only but for old people as well, and especially for very old people. That is difficult because young and old think and understand from different ends of life. Don't be afraid to interrupt me. Don't be afraid to ask me any question that comes to you. Tell me what you like and tell me what you don't like. If we are going to write this together we have to work together at the task." Not too much lecture, I thought. He squirmed in his seat as if preparing to get receptive and I started reading Chapter One.

In the first few pages, I stopped several times to qualify words or statements. "*The Inquirer* is the name of the Philadelphia newspaper. 'Hoops of steel' is in a line from Shakespeare and means that they were strongly bound to each other. The Shipman's Guild was like a union hall for seamen where they regularly met and ate together."

"I know about that. We read about a guild in one of our books at school."

I was surprised. I would have thought that 'guild' would certainly be a strange term. I continued. The word 'newfangled' was unfamiliar and I explained it by saying that the computer, and I pointed to mine, was newfangled to me even though it was part of his every-day life.

At that point he wiggled in his chair, and half put up his hand, and haltingly said, "I've got an idea."

"Go ahead," I said.

"Why don't you take those words that you think I don't know and maybe those you are not so sure I know and put them in a glossary?"

All in one "why" question Ryan had told me we were in partnership. Glossary was a word I would have bet he did not know. His question was one I might have expected from an editor who fully understood the project and knew how to make the structure allow a story that could speak to an old man and still be an adventure to a young man.

I said, "That's right! That is just the right thing to do. It gives me some freedom as an adult and keeps me from having to talk down to you. Glossary! That's just what we need." And I recognized with relief that this experience might surely have possibilities for us both.

Ryan's Glossary

aft - stern, opposite of fore as in fore and aft.

alliteration - the same sounds or letters appearing in closely connected words.

alter-ego - someone's alternate personality.

apex - a tip or pointed end.

atrophy - to die off through lack of use.

baguette - a long loaf of French bread.

banter - loose, playful conversation.

bateau - a flat bottomed boat used in shallow water.

beam - a ship's breadth at its greatest point.

belaying - wooden pin for wrapping a rope, as in belaying pin or a nautical term, stop.

berm - in this case, the top of a river bank.

bloomeries - a type of iron furnace.

bobstay - a rope used to hold down a bowsprit of a ship and keep it steady.

bouncer - person who throws out unwanted guests.

bounties - extra money given for extra service.

brig - a two-masted vessel square rigged on both masts.

buckles - in creating dyes, these were chunks of metallic lead used in the process.

buttresses - a projecting support as in a ceiling.

Caliphate - Islamic form of government as a constitutional republic.

carat - measure of the size of a precious stone.

catwater - load displacement line on a sailing ship.

cerebral - scull.

Chargé d'Affaire - French for a person officially representing a country on foreign soil.

charlatans - persons who pretend to be what they are not.

Cooper - person who makes casks, barrels, buckets or tubs.

Datu - native word for headman.

deity - a god

euphemism - a milder word used as a substitute but having the same meaning as a stronger word.

forecastle - refers to the upper deck in a sailing ship near the front.

furl - to bring in a sail or a flag.

gaff - the spar on which the fore and aft sail is extended.

imbued - to penetrate.

irony or ironic - a literary technique that goes beyond the simple, evident meaning of words.

Janus - facing in both directions as in the Roman God of gates and doorways.

jib - a triangular projecting sail.

Khedive - the same as a vice king or ruler.

Kimberlites - one of three sources of diamonds.

Know Nothings- An American Political Party that opposed immigration

Malays - people from Malaysia.

martyr - person who gives up their life for the good of others.

medallic- made in the form of a medal and affixed to something like a vase.

minarets - architectural features of Islamic mosques, tall spires with crowns.

Modus operandi - (Latin) - method of operation.

mosque - Moslem place of worship.

notoriety - fame usually from unwanted places.

octahedron - a solid figure contained by eight plane faces.

Ottoman - modern Turkish Empire.

paradox - a confusing truth that seems to contradict.

panic, as in Van Buren Panic – the result of a rapid drop in financial rates or values.

promontory- a peak or jutting rock.

quackery - unqualified practice of medicine.

reefed - strips across the sail used for rolling it up.

sarong - wrap around skirt.

scammony- a medicinal weed.

scrimshaw - engraving by whalers on mammal teeth or bone.

scrapple- a kind of liver pudding common to Pennsylvania Dutch.

score - twenty as in twenty times.

Secession - a political act of withdrawing from a contract between governments.

Sephardim - Jews whose roots go back to Spain

sepulcher- a small room cut in rock for receiving a body.

shelter board- protected area on ship.

spanker- a fore and aft sail attached to the aft side of the mizzenmast.

stoic - without emotion.

sulfur (or sulphur)- chemical element essential for life.

swashbuckling - slang for acting with excessive bravery.

Tammany Hall - a party political machine/organization in New York City.

tapers- candles

Tartan- wool cloth woven in a color pattern to indicate Clan (organization) colors.

thunderstruck - to be struck by events as if by lightening.

tragacanth - a natural gum or sap from a Middle Eastern tree.

Viziers - political advisor in a Moslem government.

vulnerable - weakened and subject to being overturned.

Whigs - a political party opposed to the Democrats.

windlass - a horizontal axle used for hauling in a sail.

About the Author

Charles D. Rodenbough, grandfather, is a writer and historian, author of four books and many articles in historical magazines and journals. This was a special project because he partnered with his grandson, **Ryan Ray Rodenbough,** who helped add the perspective of a twelve year old boy. This was Ryan's first book.

ALL THINGS THAT MATTER PRESS ™

FOR MORE INFORMATION ON TITLES AVAILABLE FROM
ALL THINGS THAT MATTER PRESS, GO TO
http://allthingsthatmatterpress.com
or contact us at
allthingsthatmatterpress@gmail.com